PRAISE FOR
Vignettes & Postcards From Morocco

"The stories in this mesmerizing collection will make you ache to travel throughout Morocco, and will sustain you until your next, or first, visit."

—Larry Habegger, executive editor,
Travelers' Tales Books

"Whether it's Jeff Greenwald's encounter with the kif-smoking Paul Bowles in Tangier, or Rolf Potts wandering a city he arrived in only by mistake, or Christina Ammon's quest for contraband Cabernet – or even the recipe you'll find for camel burger (don't forget the chopped mint) -- the contents of this book are sure to stoke your wanderlust.."

—Jim Benning, co-founder of World Hum

"Some of my favorite writers create an evocative picture of a wonderfully diverse country. It's not about where to go; it's about how to think about it when you do. This a recommended read, unless you're going there in the near future, it which case it is mandatory."

—Tim Cahill, author of *Jaguars Ripped My Flesh* and *Hold the Enlightenment*

Vignettes

&

Postcards
From Morocco

Vignettes & Postcards From Morocco

EDITOR

ERIN BYRNE

REPUTATION BOOKS

VIGNETTES & POSTCARDS FROM MOROCCO

Published by Reputation Books, LLC
reputationbooksllc.com

Copyright © 2016 by Erin Byrne

Book Design: Lisa Abellera
Photographs © Omar Chennafi, Siddharth Gupta, Christina Ammon,
Kimberley Lovato, and Anna Elkins
Sketches © Anna Elkins

ISBN 978-1-944387-06-8 (paperback)

ISBN 978-1-944387-07-5 (e-book)

First Edition: August 2016

10 9 8 7 6 5 4 3 2 1

Reputation Books

To the old man with the gentle gaze in the corner of the *souk* in the medina of Fez, Morocco: May a drop of the love with which you serve your spiced coffee to strangers be returned, overflowing, to you.

Never hesitate to go far away, beyond all seas, all frontiers, all countries, all beliefs.

—Amin Maalouf, *Leo Africanus*

The only thing that makes life worth living is the possibility of experiencing now and then a moment. And perhaps even more than that, it's having the ability to recall such moments in their totality, to contemplate them like jewels.

—Paul Bowles, *The Spider's House*

Contents

Memory

Change

Cuisine

Wisdom

Mystery

Timelessness

Introduction

Erin Byrne

A story is like water that you heat for your bath.
It takes messages between the fire and your skin.
It lets them meet, and it cleans you!
Water, stories, the body, all the things we do, are mediums
that hide and show what's hidden.
Study them, and enjoy this being washed
with a secret we sometimes know, and then not.

—Jelaluddin Rumi, from "Story Water"

MOROCCO KALEIDOSCOPES US.

We who live in, visit, write about and photograph Morocco experience a new existence: We become colorful bits, shifting in ever-blossoming shapes that twirl and twist, curl and spiral, creating patterns that dazzle even as they change.

I resisted this at first. Before arriving in Fez in spring of 2012, I'd been in Paris, orchestrating events for *Vignettes & Postcards From Paris[1]*, coaching writers on split-second

---

1   The title for the first two editions was *Vignettes & Postcards, Writings From the Evening Writing Workshop at Shakespeare and Company Bookstore,*

readings, constantly "on stage." As an introvert on overload, my thinking fuzzed, my eyes glazed; even my skin felt strained.

If one arrives in Morocco in this state, something's got to give, and it won't be the ancient city of Fez, which Leo Africanus described in the 16th century: "The roofes of their houses they adorne with golde, azure, and other excellent colours . . . golde, which mettall in the Arabian language is called Fez.[2]"

Established in the year of our Lord 786, Fez was undaunted by me. But I was, by it.

At the airport, the golden flag of my friend Christina's blonde hair bobbed among dark heads, scarves and hoods. The ride into Fez was a tawny blur of ancient arches upon hills of sand. This landscape, telescoped by time, made *me* feel faraway. We got out at Square R'Cif, where flashes of color flowed: Donkeys swayed under piles of vivid rugs, women in jewel-toned *djellabas* drifted, green and blue awnings flapped.

The *souk* vibrated in Technicolor as we squeezed between Crayola-box walls of *babouche* slippers. An onslaught of aromas hit: mint, prunes, spicy meats. Boys' shouts and staccato birdsongs rose and fell, undulated and zigzagged like *Fantasia's* Stokowski symphony.

Paris, Fall 2011 by Something Other Press. The new edition, *Vignettes & Postcards From Paris*, published by Reputation Books, will be released in August, 2016.

2   From *The History and Description of Africa: And of the Notable Things Therein Contained* by Al-Hassan Ibn-Mohammed Al-Wezaz Al-Fasi, A Moor, Baptised as Giovanni Leone, but Better Known as Leo Africanus, Done Into English in the Year 1600, London, printed for the Hakluyt Society.

We scrunched at a corner table. An old man whose narrow face tilted tenderly caressed glasses in slender fingers. His eyes were a soft embrace of blue and gray as he stooped to pour coffee laced with cinnamon, nutmeg, ginger, and anise.

This was a welcome oasis. I prefer more personal space, less interaction, and am highly—perhaps overly—attuned to any environment. In Morocco, there are multitudes of emotional undercurrents and spiritual presences—of the living and the dead. I was a prickly sponge; it hurt to absorb so much.

Around the table, the dance continued, choreographed to include every being. Even dust motes quivered frenetically as if embodied by past spirits.

After coffee, we resumed the rapids. Girls in soccer uniforms skipped past, their curls brushing my arm. A woman held up a rubbery chicken whose claw scratched my head, dead fish dripped water onto my toe, kittens rolled in a soft ball against my ankle.

Scintillating scents of rosemary, fresh leather. Heady tastes of honey: eucalyptus, orange, lavender. Colors: fuchsia, scarlet, ruby, pink. A puff of breath on my face, skin touching mine burning. Close, far, up, down, loud, hushed.

Minutes later, refuge: I lay on my back along a bench in a high-ceilinged restaurant, Café Clock, consciousness shrinking, expanding. Finally, we wended our way to Riad Zany, where friends Suzanna Clarke and Sandy McCutcheon had offered their home.

The riad, featured in Suzanna's spectacular book, *A House in Fez*, had the feel of an opulent palace. Indigo and white *zellij* tiles on the courtyard floor captured moonlight; a lemon tree arched above a silent fountain reflecting an inky sky flecked with stars.

In an upstairs room, I slept fitfully. The painted ceiling seemed to rotate in circles of diamonds and triangles, exploding then contracting in violet, green, blue—then black velvet sleep. The iron spirals covering the window curled. A sound sloshed in, a hollow keen of melancholic longing that filled me to the brim and spilled over. Grainy dawn, roosters, a dog, wheels of a rolling cart. Asleep, awake. Slanted sunlight. Down in the courtyard, footsteps on tile, the scent of toast wafting up.

The young housekeeper, Rachida, smiled shyly, radiating calm.

That week, the Fez Medina and I wrestled for control of my contours. Equilibrium vanished as soon as we entered the market-maze. Intimacy between people was palpable, and welcome was extended, but I hid behind sunglasses. The place thrummed and I heard the rhythm, until a wooden box cracked to the ground. I drifted along, then a hanging goat's head bobbed inches from my nose.

One day, we took the train to Meknès, then sardined in a car toward Moulay Idriss. We wound through a smaller medina and arrived at Scorpion House, the riad-restaurant of Mike Richardson, who owns Café Clock[3]. Mike flung open the door, beaming, in a plaid shirt, straw hat, and a reddish beard—Morocco's own Van Gogh.

---

3   Mike opened Café Clock in Marrakech in 2013.

Here, all was calm. We lingered on the terrace overlooking the medina and tree-covered hills, savoring *kefta* kebobs and couscous salad. In the distance a weary donkey brayed. Birds arced, gliding toward the sun.

—◆◆◆—

I thought of Paul Bowles' *The Spider's House,* a novel about changes—within Morocco, violently wrought by the French, within an American writer, Stenham, and a Moroccan boy, Amar. Stenham's outlines remain rigid throughout most of the story, but Amar, in the midst of turmoil in Fez, and the turbulent adolescence in his own maturing mind—is the character most open to transformation. Amar relies on Allah to change his heart when needed, and he adjusts his expectations: *The world was something different from what he had thought it. It had come nearer, but in coming nearer it had grown smaller.*

In an effort to emulate Amar, over the next day in Fez, when my body italicized itself I bended. The curlicues of calligraphy upon walls, humming of men kneeling on prayer rugs in a mosque, and cozy sense of community entered and expanded me. It was exhilarating, but ended quickly. I swore that the next time I came I'd be more prepared to acquiesce to this evolution of self.

Two years later, I returned to teach a writing workshop. Due to family crisis and a death, I again arrived in a weakened state, and the tug-of-war continued. The medina's clanging chaos yanked and I resisted. Still, some of it seeped in: Sandy and Suzanna's hospitality was gracious and Rachida's smile held the same warmth. The old man presented his coffee. In Square R'Cif, one woman in a turquoise *djellaba*, another in yellow, nestled next to each other, engrossed. A toddler raised his arms to a teenager, three boys swaggered past arm-in-arm.

In Moulay Idriss, across from Scorpion House, smoke rose from a brick chimney as a hooded figure walked across the highest rooftop, silhouetted against the sky. A ghost or a *djinn*? Again, the place issued an invitation to soak this all up, be saturated and swell.

Robert Louis Stevenson once observed, "There are no foreign lands. It is the traveler only who is foreign."

We can remain foreign, a chip hovering outside the spirographic scene, or dive in, but the world's designs will unfold with or without us.

The women sitting shoulder-to-shoulder would continue to confide, kittens to mew their skeletal way across pathways under the criss-crossed shadows of the lattice-roofed medina. Mint and sugar would mingle at the swirl of a spoon. The gentle man would serve his coffee with love. The only thing that would disappear was my chance to be a part of this action, to not just be *in* Morocco, but to move *with* it.

We returned to Fez for one more night. Christina led the group to a restaurant in a corner of the medina. People streamed past, bumping our crowded table, bringing to mind the Berbers, nomadic tribes who began wandering in 400 BC. Omar, an enthusiastic Moroccan photographer, outlined his plans for an international photography gathering, Sandy and Suzanna told local tales and friends of theirs stopped to greet us. We were in an eddy, through which the action splashed.

The next day, after reclining with one last glass of mint tea at Café Clock, we twisted and turned our way out of the medina. Every vibration tingled my skin and reverberated inside at full voltage. I was animated, alive . . . altered.

I flew to Paris, to stay at the airport hotel and depart the next morning. In the hotel room I heaved luxurious sighs. No trancelike chants or mysterious rustlings of ancient *djinns*, or cats yowling at the moon—just a bed in tidy silence. The spacious bathroom beckoned: bleach-kissed towels, pristine chrome, and a glistening white bathtub.

Hot water gushed as I poured in an entire bottle of bath gel. Lavender-scented steam rose from iridescent bubbles, which popped, spraying tiny droplets. I stripped in a flash. White sandal marks highlighted grayish sludge on my filthy feet. The grime had weight; I *felt* a drop of urine from a scraggly dog, a black arm-hair from a shopkeeper, a smear of yellow dye from the tanneries. . . . Even the sounds, smells and tastes clung to me: My ears rang with the thump of rugs being stacked, the path from my nose to my head burned with the dizzy sweetness of stewed lemons, syrupy honey clogged my throat.

Once in, I lathered and scrubbed and rinsed and rubbed. Dirt separated into brown granules and sank. A turquoise thread bounced atop the suds, a miniature white hair (kitten? eyelash?) and a tiny purple crescent of a *zellij* whorled in the now-brownish water. I turned the lever; the drain rumbled.

Lushshshshs. The last of the water carrying the bright specks circled toward the cylindrical pipe that would whisk it all away. A silver fish scale; a sliver of emerald mint; a particle of donkey dung from a gentle, droopy-eyed creature; a microscopic cell from Rachida's hand which had touched the top of mine when we said goodbye. As the whirlpool disappeared, I realized something:

I wanted it all back.

I wanted Morocco to stop rushing away, to return to my body. I longed to follow it all down the drain—even that which was as fleeting as Rachida's shyness, as intangible as Omar's eye for symmetry, as invisible as the air of intimacy that pervaded all of it—for I had only just begun to add my own heartbeat to the pulse of Morocco.

This book brings it back.

The stories, poems, photographs and sketches that vibrate inside this book invite us to move with Morocco as each writer does. Rolf Potts meanders in Tetouan, and James Dorsey is chased through Marrakech. Kimberley Lovato and Marcia DeSanctis whirl into memory and Jeff Greenwald traverses decades in his conversation with Paul Bowles.

Suzanna and Sandy, Omar, and Mike, who mingle with Morocco every day, bring us its children, its beliefs, its scenes and cuisines.

Michael Chabon and his family rattle around on hidden roads in Zegota, and stop for a meal in an unlikely place. Phil Cousineau taps out a new beat, and Paul Bowles himself leads us into the Sahara.

To an endless refrain of prayers and brays, as the *chergui,* desert wind, repeatedly whips reality into fantasy, and the perpetually full tea glass caresses its minty bouquet. . . . from Casablanca to Tangier, from the crush of Marrakech to the ethereal solitude of the Sahara, from a rose festival in the countryside to a betrothal fair high in the Atlas Mountains, in alleyways and on rooftops, we rotate in a dervish-dance with Morocco.

May these stories from inside the spiral toss and tumble your imagination so that you feel your own essence touched, your edges jostled, your colors deepen—until you become a shape-shifting gem and spin with us, with Morocco, creating unending patterns of green and blue and azure . . . and gold.

Erin Byrne

June, 2015

Arrival

A little imagination goes a long way in Fez.
—Tahir Shah, *Travels with Myself*

Welcome to Morocco

Sandy McCutcheon

Deep Travel Celebration
March, 2014, Riad Zany, Fez

THEY CAME SEEKING WORDS and images, sounds and sights and smells. They came from the new to the old. Here they would find what they sought.

For, from the cracks in the *zellij* emerged words. New words, their sounds unfamiliar. Words from every wall and stone, from dark doorways, from narrow lanes and alleys. The language was not theirs. Consonants coruscating beneath a crescent moon. Vowels that melded with such grace and ease that it took their breath away. Trees sighed and behind walls hidden court-yards bequeathed the tinkling language of fountain and spring, water and mist blessed by the laughter of children, the tapping and subtle shuttle clicking of artisans and a lone woman on a rooftop ululating her thanks for some unknown joy. In the nests atop mosques and minarets the onomatopoeic Lac Lac clicks its invitation to its chicks to feed only to be drowned out by the advancing tsunami of sound that is the call to prayer. "*Alu O Akbar*" comes the cry repeatedly ringing, resonating, ricocheting off the tiles.

Pause for a moment and wonder at what the words of the medina are telling you, for these syllables contain within the ancient magic of the Amazigh, the Berber, the *aguzas*; the witches and the *dejoun*—the *djinns* that share this space between night and day.

Try not to understand the words. This wild magic, whispered in a foreign tongue is not to be comprehended, but absorbed by osmosis and later to infuse your own words with new and subtle power. The medina gives you these words. They are a gift. Subtle as sun showers, brilliant as starlight and as precious as a smile from the beloved.

Imaginary Countries

Sabrina Crawford

MOROCCO—THREE SYLLABLES roll from o to c, c to o driven forth from a thousand ancient tongues to the ear of the world. Morocco—desert king of imaginary cities—a libertine maze of jagged, dusty, switchback zigzag zagzig pathways, each harboring a hundred hidden secrets.

Morocco—land of the bazaar, vendor calls and shouts, shouts and calls, the rhythmic hypno beat of hand against drum, drum against hand, pulse, pulse pulsing all day long. Morocco—land of donkeys braying, mint tea wafting, plates of dates and olives piled high in stall after stall after stall. Morocco—land of the siren call to prayer not once, not twice, but five times a day, when the faithful bend their minds and bodies toward Mecca.

Morocco. We've not even yet arrived here and already we're lost.

In between past and present, now and then, then and now, Morocco sits, waiting for us, a country of two faces: one real, one imaginary. The latter we know, the other, a shape-shifting mystery we wait to encounter. Twenty thousand feet careening high above the edges of Europe, waiting to cross over into Africa, we head toward her.

In our mind's pockets we carry her twin sister's photo, the bright burning image of this dreamy-eyed other. How will one look placed side-by-side with the other? The real next to the imaginary?

Morocco the imaginary is *my* Morocco. Each traveler snaps and carries her own. My Morocco is the mythic dreamland of Marco Polo—the promise of mystery, the explorer's journey into the unknown. My Morocco sails a fleet of ten thousand ships into the dark waters of memory through a hundred haunted hashish-filled hallucinogenic dreams into make-believe Marrakech markets filled with snake charmers, Sufi poets and drums that beat, beat, beat all night long.

My Morocco is the mountain land of Paul Bowles, Brian Jones and William S. Burroughs—of poets and wanderers, whose ghostly figures still roam the crooked streets at night, crying out, searching for a home away from home.

It's the land of outsiders and renegades, misfits and mystics, poets and rock stars—modern explorers. Their footsteps, songs and images guide me, drawing a map on my heart of a place that does not exist—and yet endures.

My Morocco is a crystal palace rising deep in the heart of the desert, surrounded by mountains, encased by legend upon legend, century upon century of kings and pashas, conquerors and emperors, Berbers, Jews and Moors.

As we dive 10,000 feet swooping closer and closer to earth, I kiss goodbye to the edges of Europe. Here at the Straits of Gibraltar, I see for an instant the edge of the world. Here I cross over like so many before.

Here together we pilgrims set forth to knock at Africa's front door—having traveled thousands of miles through imaginary lands to arrive at long last at the real Morocco—like so many before and before and before.

The "I" of Morocco

Anna Elkins

For Ali, who explained my name to me

In Arabic, my name means *I*.
Ana this, *ana* that.
I am called everywhere,
but I am not meant.
So I surrender to the collective self—
I in the *souk* selling oranges
       with their leaves on.
I in the café filled with men
     wondering at a woman.
I in the tannery lifting skins
       through vats of urine.
I in the child kicking a faded ball

down a medina street.
I in the man pointing to a pastry
with a bee stuck in sugar.
I in the *petit-taxi* holding out
a creased hand for coins.
I in the woman rubbing cheese
onto squares of fry bread.
I in the singers with blank faces
on the brink of desert.
I in the shepherd telling the sheep
his dreams.
Now, the world turns *ana*—
I am the river running beneath
the ancient city,
over mountains,
to the sands.
I am dunes, pink in evening.
I am the sky above them as night falls.
The sky—wider than lives,
spacious enough to hold every hand
and turn each finger to a star
that points all *I's* home.

Vignettes

Because we don't know when we will die, we get to think of life as an inexhaustible well. Yet everything happens only a certain number of times, and a very small number, really. How many more times will you remember a certain afternoon of your childhood, an afternoon that is so deeply a part of your being that you can't even conceive of your life without it? Perhaps four, five times more, perhaps not even that. How many more times will you watch the full moon rise? Perhaps twenty. And yet it all seems limitless.

—Paul Bowles, *The Sheltering Sky*

Oranges in Marrakech, Sweetness in Fez, and Bowles in Tangier

Excerpted from *The Size of the World*

Jeff Greenwald

Author's note: In 1993 and 1994 I circled the world overland, traveling only by land and sea. Leaving the continent by ship from Brooklyn, I came ashore in Senegal—and from there made my way through Mali, Mauritania and Western Sahara to Morocco. These three excerpts are from the book about that visit.

Oranges in Marrakech

THE WORD 'FRUIT' WAS inadequate to convey the richness of Marrakech's urban arbors. It wasn't a question of a few stray globes hanging over the clean sidewalks. Banquets of oranges weighted the limbs of the trees lining Avenue Mohammed V, fluorescent against red clay walls, ripening patiently against an animated backdrop of buses, taxis and horse-drawn cabs.

Though the medina was spectacular, it was not where I worshipped. Just to the west of the Jamaa el Fna—the inscrutably-named "Place of Nothing" where the clowns and dentists and storytellers perform—the city's orange-sellers ply their trade. There are dozens of them, positioned behind broad wooden tables sagging under the weight of their cargo. Millions of huge, sweet oranges, the pride of Morocco, rise in four-sided pyramids toward the sky, half obscuring the red-cheeked, thick-wristed men who split and pump them dry in tough chrome squeezers. For two *dirhams*—18 cents—one is handed a tall clean glass filled to the brim with fresh, cold orange juice so perfect and honest and sweet that you burst into tears drinking it. Here, at last, is the Platonic ideal, and everything you've had before—everything else called "orange juice"—has been but a lame attempt to imitate it. *Thank God for oranges,* you cry, downing your first glass. *Thank God for Morocco, and the planet Earth!* After two glasses you are deliriously happy; after six glasses you're whirling like a dervish, spinning wildly through the Jamaa el Fna, spinning in a beatific citrus ecstasy while blind Moroccan beggars toss coins into the empty glass still clutched in your spinning hand. . . .

SWEETNESS IN FEZ

Confusion, for more than a moment, is not possible in Fez. People instantly materialize to assist you—whether out of altruism or for profit one doesn't always know for sure. In a place like the medina all offers are suspect; elsewhere the motivation is sometimes completely pure.

The man found me inside the gate of the Hebrew Cemetery, a tilting acre of whitewashed geometrical tombs attached to the southeastern fringe of the Fez *Mellah*. I had come to light a memorial candle for my brother, who had taken his life four years ago to the day.

There was no point pretending I didn't need help. I was seen wandering around in befuddlement, looking for something that might be a synagogue.

"Vous cherchez quelque chose?"

He was not one of those ageless Moroccans. White hair ebbed back from his forehead in two pronounced U's, and a short white moustache formed a hedge beneath his nose. It was a nose with real personality; the sort of nose that had probably brought him grief as a child, but had matured into a distinguished asset. I couldn't see his eyes through his sunglasses.

"Is there a synagogue here?"

"No, no . . ." He removed his glasses to polish them with a handkerchief, and I put him at fifty. "There is no synagogue here. In the Ville Nouvelle." He gestured with his chin, back toward the bridge I'd crossed to get where I was. "There are not many Jews in the *Mellah* anymore. When the French built the New City many moved there. Or to Palestine. There are many Jews in Rabat. And Casablanca."

"Is there any place," I asked, "where I might light a memorial candle? My brother died four years ago this month, and I wish to recite the *Kaddish* for him."

He nodded quickly—"Wait a moment"—and walked off to speak with an elderly black caretaker. They returned together. "Give this man some money, and he can bring you what you need: candles, matches, and a *yarmulke* to cover your head."

"How much?"

"Five *dirhams*."

I handed the black man a coin, and he left through the cemetery gate.

"If there's no synagogue," I asked my companion, "where do I light the candle?"

He put a hand on my shoulder and pointed. Most of the tombs in the cemetery were similar: low, whitewashed half-cylinders rising from the ground.

There were two, though, that stood higher than the rest. One was a loaf-shaped shrine (like a big baguette with the ends cut off) covered in shiny, black tile. A smoke pipe rose from one end. It looked like a cartoon locomotive and, when I first saw it, I actually thought it was the custom-built tomb of a Jew who had spent a lifetime on the railroad. The second shrine was plainer. White and symmetrical, it had an opening in one side and a tall, blackened chimney.

It was those two structures that my friend indicated. "There, and there," he said. "Light your candles inside, away from the wind."

"Why are there two?"

He shrugged. "We call them the Father and the Mother."

The caretaker returned with a rose-patterned skullcap, a box of wooden matches and a wrapped paper package containing six kosher candles. He handed me my change.

The white-haired man led me toward the black-tiled shrine, which I assumed was the one they called 'the Father.' Along the way he pointed out memorial placards: Jews who had died during the Second World War; the graves of children; the oldest tombs, inscribed exclusively in Hebrew, with no French translation. We stopped for a moment before a memorial to a seventeen-year-old girl, killed by the Arabs when she refused to convert to Islam.

When we reached the high black tomb with its open candle-well in the center, the man stood beside me with his hands folded. I lit three candles and uttered what little I could remember of the *Kaddish*. When my *yarmulke* blew off in a strong breeze, the man chased after it and returned it to me. I put it quickly to my lips. When I was convinced the candles were secure from the wind we walked over to the white 'Mother' shrine; I lit my remaining candles there.

Afterwards we rested on a gray marble bench beneath an orange tree. Fallen fruit filled the shallow square well protecting the trunk. On an impulse—and because I trusted him somehow—I told the man of the circumstances of Jordan's death. He confided that his own brother had also died four years ago, at the age of forty. He himself was forty-seven.

"How large is the Jewish community here in Fez?" I asked.

The man shrugged. "Most are in the Ville Nouvelle, where the synagogue is. It's difficult to say."

"How many do you think? Twenty families? Fifty? One hundred?"

"More than one hundred."

"And what about marriage? Do Jews often intermarry with Muslims?"

He held out his flattened palm and tilted it from side to side. "They do."

"That's unusual," I said.

"Not really. In Morocco there is a long history of compatibility between Jews and Muslims. We live together without racism, without prejudice. Jews and Muslims grow up in the same neighborhoods; often our families live so close together that we are like cousins. Jews will have many Arab friends, and Arabs will have many Jewish friends. And once every year— this coming weekend, in fact—the Arabs will visit the Jewish homes and buy bread from them."

"Buy bread?"

"*Bien sûr.* It is the time of year when bread is forbidden in the Jewish homes."

"Of course. I'm sorry. Passover."

"Exactly."

I took a picture of the man sitting on the bench, the gravestones of the Jewish cemetery arrayed behind him, the mosques of Djemma el Bali rising in the distance. He had a pleasant, reserved smile, and seemed perfectly content to while away the afternoon in the cemetery.

I asked, "Will your Muslim friends visit your home this Saturday?" He looked confused. "To buy bread." He continued to regard me blankly. "As you mentioned. Do you keep the Passover?"

"Ahh!" His face lit up, and as he smiled I saw that there were still black hairs in his moustache. "No, no . . ."

"You'll go to a seder elsewhere, then?"

He shook his head and reached out to shake my hand—Morocco's universal gesture of agreement, amity and amusement. "Not this year," he said.

I held his hand and returned his smile. "Why not?"

"Because I am Muslim," he replied, "and we do not celebrate the Passover."

Paul Bowles in Tangier

The feeling in Tangier is that anything is possible. Not as it was in the 1950s, perhaps, but possible nonetheless. In some ways the city feels like the northern edge of San Francisco: white buildings and long stairways clustering down steep hills that terminate at the docks and the sea. Tangier was the original Barbary Coast, and though time has tamed its deadlier appetites there remains the growl of unrequited hunger and a taste for the indecent. And Tangier, like San Francisco, is a city of action. Vehicles—ships, trains, taxis and ferries—are continually on the move. The streets are thick with pedestrians. Fish fry hurriedly in narrow outdoor cafés. Boys with acne-scarred faces cast their nets from doorways, peddling sex and hashish.

Ahamed, a native of Tangier, had been a guide for almost thirty years. He'd been to author Paul Bowles' flat a few dozen times, usually bringing foreign journalists, Beat groupies or other curiosity seekers. His most recent visit had occurred about a year and a half before. Since that time, Ahamed warned me, Bowles' health had deteriorated; he could get me to the writer's apartment, but offered no guarantee of an audience.

Bowles' apartment consists of four rooms. I entered through the front door, passing a small kitchen on my right, and traversed a living room—the largest room in the house—with dark curtains drawn. Half a dozen *kilims* covered the floor, and there was a low sofa. A coffee table sat in the center of the room, covered with art books. Against the left wall stood a bookshelf filled with editions and translations of works by both Paul and his wife Jane Bowles, who died of cancer in 1973. Beside the bookshelf was a compact stereo with stacks of CDs piled on the floor around it.

The far right corner of the living room ended in a square nook with three doors. The door to the left opened into Bowles' study. I couldn't resist peering inside. It was a veritable shrine to the printed word, with three walls hidden by sagging bookshelves. The fourth wall held a huge picture window which, facing east, admitted a broad panorama of the hills and illuminated buildings beyond his neighborhood.

The central door led into the boudoir, lit by an incandescent table lamp. Every inch of the small bedroom was spoken for. Clothes were heaped on the bureau. Two portable stereos and a collection of recordings sat below the shuttered window. Books littered the floor, sat in sliding piles beneath the dresser, edged off the table, infiltrated the chaos of the bureau, congregated under the bed.

The author of *The Sheltering Sky* lay between black paisley sheets, propped on a pillow, wrapped in a pale-brown, felt robe. A bed table bridged his lap; upon this rested his tea, a few gelatin capsules, a lighter and a hand-painted cigarette case filled with *kif* cigarettes.

A circular table in the center of the room was loaded with balms and medicines—an arsenal against the eighty-three-year-old writer's plethora of ailments. Bowles lay in his bed, his physical frailty belied by his sharp gaze and immediate wit. I shook his hand.

"I'm Paul Bowles," he informed me, so that there would be no confusion.

My chair was on the other side of the table. Bowles, his books and myself formed a constellation in the close atmosphere of the room. I placed the lily I had bought on the table. A moment later, flustered, I stood up to shake his hand again.

"You don't remember," he laughed, "because I gave you only one finger last time. This time I'll give you three."

Bowles' face looked long in the photographs I'd seen, but framed between the pillows and the folds of his nightshirt it appeared compact, even gnomic. Deep furrows ran alongside his nose. His eyes were large, blue and very focused. He may have been in pain—he'd recently had surgery to remove a tumor from behind his right ear, and his legs were giving him trouble— but if so it did not register in his face. He appeared completely at ease, immediately engaging and marginally flattered to be a site of pilgrimage on my round-the-world journey.

"I certainly hope you didn't come," he said suspiciously, "to meet the grandfather of the Beat writers."

"Well, that would probably be Burroughs," I said. "Anyway, you're not a Beat writer."

"You're right." He nodded approvingly, as if I'd passed a test. "I never was. But people get that confused. All those pictures of Ginsberg and so forth in Tangier. But I never was a Beat writer, no. I love the English language too much. I was always too . . . I don't want to say literate. . . . I was always too *literary.*"

Bowles, born in 1910, grew up in New York City. During the 1930s he lived for a time in Paris, meeting Alexander Calder and rooming briefly with Gertrude Stein (who, claiming that all Americans stank, forced him to take cold baths). Though he's best known as a novelist and short-story writer, Bowles first achieved notoriety as a composer. He studied music with Aaron Copland and as a young man made good money writing music for Broadway shows. He also served as music critic for the now defunct *Herald-Tribune*—an experience that led directly, he claimed, to his ability to tackle the challenge of writing a novel.

"I liked doing all that," he said, lighting a *kif* cigarette. "It was fun. But in order to do it I had to live in New York. And I was getting fed up with the life in New York.

Bowles moved to North Africa in the late 1940s. He was immediately fascinated by Morocco—a place that seemed to break all the rules—and still recalled the first time he tried to mail a letter home.

"I went into the post office and asked for a dozen airmail stamps, and the clerk told me how much they cost, and I said, 'Really? That much?' And he said, 'Okay, how much you pay?' It was the first place I'd been where you even had to bargain for postage stamps."

His first novel, *The Sheltering Sky*, was published to critical acclaim in 1949—one year before his fortieth birthday. He'd celebrated by buying a Jaguar convertible; not a bad vehicle for cruising the mountains of Morocco.

When I returned the next day, our interview became more personal.

"Yesterday," I said, "you said that words were your ammunition, your 'bullets.' I was surprised to hear you use that allegory."

Bowles shrugged, his open robe hitching on his shoulders. "Well, in defensive terms, sure. Words can be seen as bullets. I've always seen them that way. What do you defend yourself with, if you're a sedentary type? You've got nothing to shoot at people except words."

"Why 'defend' yourself at all? Anyway, that's a rather *offensive* kind of approach."

He lifted his owlish eyebrows. "Is it?"

"I think so. I've never thought of words in terms of weaponry. During our conversation yesterday you just seemed so fed up with that whole aspect of humanity. The aggression, the violence . . ."

"Well, of course. But it seems to me that you do have to defend yourself, you know?"

"Against what?"

"Against the world. The world which is inevitably attacking you. That may be paranoia, but I feel that any creative artist is an enemy of society. I think you have to . . . Well, I don't know that I consider that the entire world is against me now, but people are so likely to misunderstand everything. I mean in your writing. In *my* writing. And then they accuse me of the strangest things. I think most people resent being accused, without knowing of what. If you're a writer, you have nothing at your disposal except words. And that determines your attitude toward words; toward what one does with words. One uses them, hopefully, to express ideas. It's not always easy to put ideas into words. But if you try hard enough you can do it, of course. That's what I mean by ammunition."

Bowles began complaining of an ache in his right foot. I offered to massage it, but he asked me to just pull the sock off instead. I removed the argyle sock and studied his foot—pale and venous—thinking about the fragile corporeal container that serves, for a short time, to schlep our brains around.

"I hope I'm not overstepping my bounds," I said, "but I'd like to ask you—do you think much about death?"

He nodded, more in response to his willingness to answer than as an affirmative. "It doesn't worry me. What worries me is pain. All I want is a quiet death, without writhing around. But you never know what you're going to get.

"Actually, death . . . There's no such thing. It doesn't exist. One ceases to function, but the existence of death can't possibly be perceived. Therefore it doesn't exist."

"Do you see something beyond death?"

"No." He shook his head emphatically.

"You don't believe in life after death, or reincarnation?"

"Why should I? How could I?" He regarded me quizzically. "No. I don't go in for mysticism. It's a kind of superstition."

There was a brief silence. I asked, "Do you expect anything more from yourself creatively?"

He looked at me like I was crazy. "I never had expected anything."

"What motivates you, then? What drives you on?"

"An idea. A possible situation. It's a *game*, writing." He adjusted his legs beneath the blankets, wincing. "You play it with yourself, of course. You set yourself certain goals and try to make the result what you imagined it. You can do it with words; you can't do it with anything else. And if you're a thinker—someone who can deal with abstraction, comfortably, which I cannot—you can decide beforehand what you're going to do. But I've never been able to do that. Neither in a given work, or in my life in general. I don't like plans," Bowles said. "I never knew why people have them."

"I suppose that's true," I said. "You mentioned yesterday that you were always willing to change, to do what seemed right at the time. You had invested a tremendous amount in your identity as a composer. And yet you allowed that identity to shift, to change, without clinging to a concept of yourself as a person whose whole life was music."

Bowles lit a *kif* cigarette before replying.

"Smells like a pretty fragrant mixture you're smoking there . . ."

"That's not a mixture," Bowles replied testily. "It's pure *kif*. Marijuana. I can't smoke tobacco. That's why my leg is bad; if you smoke a lot, which I used to do, your arteries and veins can become restricted.

"But back to your question. No, I never thought that way. I never thought my life was *anything*. In fact I didn't think about my life. I lived. I tried to live; to eat and so on, though I never had any money. Sometimes I had an inheritance, a small sum, which helped a lot, especially if you're living abroad, where the dollar is good and local currency isn't. But I didn't have any concept about having a *life*; or a career, or whatever that is, no. I thought I must do what I'm supposed to do, that's it. What I *think* I'm supposed to do. And I knew that I had to eat for the energy to be able to do it."

The mention of his avatar as a composer put me in the mood for some music, and I asked if I might hear some recordings from his New York days. We drank tea and listened to a recording of his *Concerto for Two Pianos, Winds and Percussion* (1947) and a few more of his compositions.

Presently Bowles slept. I wandered into his study, and watched the paschal moon rise over the hills of Jebala.

Caressing the Weave

Leyla Giray Alyanak

I SLIDE INTO THE MAZE TO hide from the scalding sun but it follows me, playing hide and seek through the rotting wood slats over my head, painting hot stripes on my feet, on the street, on every stall.

The Fez Medina tries to push its treasures, enticing me with finely engraved brass and polished wood, with tan and crimson bags whose soft skins were fresh just an hour ago.

It calls me with its olives, green and violet, lemony and raw, plucked from trees planted by ancestors all those lifetimes past.

It seduces me with honey-coated pastries sprinkled with almonds and sprayed with the finest of powdered sugars.

Most often, this medieval mall tries to sell me its crown jewel: a lush, silky carpet of strands gathered long ago by strong women's hands, or by the delicate fingers of children who could have been sitting in a classroom.

I don't need to buy a carpet.

I breathe deeply the sweet scent of centuries of encrusted tea and pastries, the sour tang of nearby tanneries, the aroma of cardamom and cinnamon, of mint and honey, and dust from decades in forgotten corners.

I vibrate to the banging of metal on metal, iron hammer-heads shaping giant copper pots. A light wind whistles through the crooked alley, so narrow a heavily-laden donkey scrapes the sandy walls on either side.

"Please, please come, *s'il vous plait.* You speak French? German?"

A few carpet-sellers twirl, chant, gesture, pulling me into the shops and stalls I have tried so hard to avoid.

I don't need to buy a carpet, but sometimes I accept the invitation and listen to his—always a he—humble stories of wounds and death, of bankruptcy and hunger, expertly woven to tug at my guilt. Mint tea appears, sugary with dark bits of floating leaf, an offering—or perhaps a bribe.

Carpets slide out of tall, dense stacks. Young men place them gently before me, like proud pupils showing off perfect homework. Small, larger, giant-sized, they are layered astutely, a corner of each silky rectangle easily visible, arranged with the subtle geometry of sales.

My eyes flitter, gripped by the cerises and crimsons, the indigoes and ceruleans, the silver and ash, an architecture of squares and triangles and labyrinths, the geometry of Islam, of the Atlas Mountains, of centuries of roaming loosely across the land.

I don't want to buy a carpet. But I want to be near them.

Oriental carpets tug the threads of my primeval memories, yellowing images of nomads in single file, exhausted until they reach the *caravanserai* to trade what they'd transported across the desert for so many days. I imagine my forebears, turbaned and camelled, bargaining hard for a fistful of salt or a bag of juicy dates that would permit their ancient convoys to reach the next palm oasis.

When hard sell and guilt fail to budge me, the salesman's charm takes over. Workmanship is praised, this 'unique' carpet, a 'once in a lifetime opportunity.' An older woman crouches in a corner, a smoothly woven shawl covering her head and shoulders, her rough hands held up as evidence of the loving care she has threaded into each luscious tapestry.

Every effort to part me from my cash will fail, as I am only here to rub and smell, to run my hands over the silk and the wool as though the carpets would fly me home, through centuries and continents, to ancestors stretching as far as the stars.

The carpet shop owner looks at me, expectantly, with hope. I am far away, lost in soft memory.

Eventually he is convinced I am a looker, not a buyer.

We settle into the moment.

I learn about Said's immigration woes, Ahmed's spendthrift twin brother, Mehmed's German girlfriend who will join him soon, soon.

I learn about Fatima's arthritis, about how hard it is for her to sit at the loom and how she is training her niece to take over. Another Fatima.

I learn that the best goat cheese comes from Aliya, through the alley, around the corner, past the meat shop, down the narrow stairway to the left. And next to Aliya is a shop where I will taste olives from heaven.

Even today, the medina is a gathering place where news is shared and remembered. It is a school, a mall, a restaurant, a gallery, a social club, a job. It is, for many Fassi, the center of the universe, a *caravanserai*, an oasis. It is home, a home many find no reason to ever leave.

I don't need to buy a carpet.

I just need to caress its weave, as I would caress my mother's cheek if she were still with me. And my grandmother's.

I follow, follow those threads all the way back.

Accidental Flâneur

Rolf Potts

SINCE I TRY TO BE THE KIND of guy who can admit his mistakes, I'll say this up front: My first act upon arriving in Morocco from Spain was to mispronounce the name of my destination while arranging a long-haul taxi from the ferry-port at Tangier. Hence, instead of traveling to the town of Chefchaouen in the Rif Mountains, I ended up in the city of Tetouan, near the Mediterranean Sea. I swear this is not as dumb of a mix-up as it looks on paper.

Of the many thrills travel can offer, one of my favorites is the simple joy of moving from one new place to another. I had departed Algeciras, Spain that morning high on the prospect of crossing the Straits of Gibraltar by ferry and getting my first taste of Morocco. This buzz continued as my friend Justin and I arranged a taxi out of Tangier and up the Moroccan coast. The plan was to hit Chefchaouen, a picturesque old backpacker haunt with a reputedly laid-back vibe, by mid-afternoon.

Justin actually did the taxi negotiation (I was off checking for buses), so he made the initial mistake of saying "Chefchaouen" with two syllables and Anglophone pronunciation ("Chef-chwan") instead of the more accurate three-syllable/French pronunciation ("Shef-sha-wan"). When the taxi driver replied with the name of another two-syllable town—"Tetouan?" ("Tet-wan")—Justin nodded, a price was settled, I was waved over, and we were off. Sadly, I cannot blame the mix-up entirely on Justin, since he immediately noticed that the directional signs along the highway were pointing to "Tetouan," not "Chefchaouen"—and I responded with some tedious pedantic spiel about how, as with Hindi or Hangul or Cyrillic, there are multiple ways of transliterating the Arabic writing system into Roman letters. Had I been a little less high on the notion of rolling through an exotic new landscape (and a little more attentive to the ways of four-vowel French diphthongs), I might have paid more attention to my own lecture and realized that Justin's concern was valid.

In less than an hour (another warning sign: Chefchaouen is not that close to Tangier), the cab driver steered us into a medium-sized city not far from the coast and asked us where we wanted to be dropped off. I told him a gate to the medina (old city) called "Bab Souk," and when he said "Bab Tout?" I shrugged at the monosyllabic simplicity of the word and said yes. Look on a map, and you will see that the old city of Chefchaouen does not have a "Bab Tout." To grasp the scope of my mistake, you'd have to imagine a Moroccan Celtics fan optimistically convincing himself he was in Boston upon hearing the phrase "Madison Square Garden."

Justin and I entered the medina through Bab Tout and wandered the old city for upwards of an hour before a Belgium-born innkeeper named Jean-Marc kindly informed us that we were still a good hour way from Chefchaouen. Tetouan, where we were standing at that moment, was a town ten times the size of our presumed destination. Though less popular with foreign tourists than Chefchaouen, he said, Tetouan was fascinating in its own right: It has an extensive old market and medina studded with low, cube-like white houses; it is surrounded by almond, orange, and pomegranate orchards; it had a historical reputation as an operating base for pirates preying on Mediterranean shipping; it was rejuvenated in the 15th century by Muslims and Jews kicked out of Spain during the Inquisition.

Jean-Marc suggested I stick around for a few hours and get to know the place better, and that's just what I did, using an old travel strategy I like to call "Walk Until the Day Becomes Interesting": Instead of starting out with a list of goals or attractions for a given destination, I opt instead to find an intriguing neighborhood and wander around until something catches my eye.

In this way, my instincts become my guidebook—and it can be fun to see what happens (good and bad).

Novel as this manner of spontaneous sightseeing might sound, it's actually a time-honored travel practice—not dissimilar, in fact, to the French *flâneur* tradition of wandering the streets of Paris in search of small details and experiences. As the 19th century French poet Charles Baudelaire wrote:

> For the perfect *flâneur*, for the passionate observer, it's an immense pleasure to take up residence in multiplicity, in whatever is seething, moving, evanescent and infinite: you're not at home, but you feel at home everywhere; you see everyone, you're at the center of everything yet you remain hidden from everybody—these are just a few of the minor pleasures of those independent, passionate, impartial minds whom language can only awkwardly define. . . . The amateur of life enters into the crowd as into an immense reservoir of electricity.

The traditional French *flâneur* doesn't see his wandering as a purely touristic act (by definition, he's exploring his own city) but it's an interesting comparison: Freed of expectations, a person can wander into a new environment with the sense that anything might happen. As an outsider I certainly wasn't "hidden from everybody" in Morocco, but I love the idea of being a "passionate observer," of being an "amateur of life" experiencing small moments of electricity in novel surroundings.

As accidental discoveries go, my timing couldn't have been better, since farmers and merchants from the surrounding mountains were taking advantage of a once-a-month tax-break for ethnic-Berber vendors: Tetouan's narrow market alleyways were jammed with women in colorful costumes selling little piles of spices and onions and goat meat. As I walked through the medina, I got the sense that the Berbers were as stoked to be there as I was: They, too, were travelers, visiting the "big city" from their isolated homes in the countryside.

Before long I was accosted by Bilal, a local nineteen-year-old who claimed he wanted to practice his English with us. Having traveled in similar countries (like Egypt) before, I knew that a) it would be hard to get rid of Bilal, and b) he hadn't approached us to practice his English, but rather to steer us into jewelry shops and leatherwork kiosks in the hopes of scoring a commission. Bilal was harmless enough, as touts go, and eventually I agreed to let him guide us through the market. My only condition was that we remain in the Berber-merchant area, and that we not end up in a carpet shop.

There is perhaps no greater testament to the powers of Moroccan charm and persuasion than the fact that I found myself in a carpet showroom approximately thirteen minutes later.

The carpet shop was owned by a genial, *djellaba*-wearing old fellow named Mustafa, who Bilal claimed (rather unconvincingly) as a distant uncle. The moment I walked into Mustafa's showroom, he started in on an intricately choreographed presentation-routine worthy of a TV shopping channel. Despite my repeated claims that I had no interest in buying a carpet, Mustafa just shot me a winsome grin and spouted carpet facts (how the red hue comes from poppies; how the finest wool is from the neck of the lamb) while three employees raced around unrolling rugs and theatrically caressing the merchandise.

Mustafa's pitch, which appeared to be memorized, included everything from Vaudeville-style jokes ("Look at how generous we are: If you buy you pay only for one side; the other side is free"); to Berber ethnography ("traditionally, these carpets are presented as tribal wedding gifts"); to the earnestly asserted conviction that I could buy a truckload of his rugs, saunter into Bloomingdale's department store in Manhattan, and sell them for an enormous profit (which, Mustafa hinted, could then be used to buy more of his rugs). "If there's room in your heart," his refrain went, "there's room in your house."

I eventually convinced Mustafa that my heart was a stubbornly minimalist place that had no room at the moment for Moroccan handicrafts, and he was quite the good sport about it ("If I stopped trying to sell every time a tourist said they didn't come to Morocco for a rug," he said, "I would not have a business any more").

After Mustafa's shop I was beginning to think I'd give Chefchaouen a miss and stay the night in Tetouan—but by this point Bilal had taken it upon himself to find Justin and me a ride up to our initial destination, and we didn't have much luck in convincing him we were no longer interested. With the help of a guy named Rasheed (a friend of Bilal's who sported a rugby shirt that said "Oakland Athletics" on the front and "Chicken Gourmet" on the back), we found a taxi driver named Mohammed who agreed to make the one-hour drive to Chefchaouen.

Bilal and Rasheed tagged along for the road-trip, which featured blow-dryer-hot air streaming in through the windows, and a number of blind-curve passing maneuvers (one of which involved an over-laden propane truck) as we wound our way up into the Rif mountains. After paying Mohammed for his dare-devil driving services (and tipping Bilal for his at-times dubious guide-service), Justin and I hit Chefchaouen's old town for some more adventure.

As it turned out, however, the tidy medina of Chefchaouen (a gentrified old hippie haunt, similar to San Miguel de Allende in Mexico, or Matala in Crete) was a letdown after our afternoon in Tetouan's old town. Chefchaouen featured lovely blue alleyways, tasteful handicraft shops, and peaceful travelers' tea-houses—but we'd been spoiled by the heady buzz of mild chaos that results when you show up at the wrong place and walk until the day becomes interesting.

Memory

I think it is all a matter of love; the more you love a memory the stronger and stranger it becomes.

—Vladimir Nabokov

And never forget that writing is as close as we get to keeping a hold on the thousand and one things—childhood, certainties, cities, doubts, dreams, instants, phrases, parents, loves—that go on slipping, like sand, through our fingers.

—Salman Rushdie, *Imaginary Homelands: Essays and Criticism 1981-1991*

Sister

Kimberley Lovato

LAHSSAN STREAMS HOT TEA from an ornate silver pot into a colored glass stuffed with fresh mint leaves and sugar cubes, and sets it on the table.

"This is your last night in Maroc, Sister. What you think?" he asks in accented English, using the French word for Morocco and the name he's called me since we first met.

"I've fallen under the spell," I say. "I especially love your city of Fez and can't wait to return."

Lahssan's brows press together at my brisk speech. I repeat the words slowly, eliminating the idiomatic expression.

His eyes spark with comprehension and a smile spreads across his cheeks as he places a blue and white plate of cookies in front of me then puts his hand over his heart.

"You are most welcome Sister," he says.

Dressed in a burgundy-hued traditional *djellaba* and white leather slippers, he shuffles through a doorway and out of sight.

Back home, being called "Sister" by anyone other than my brother would have felt as threadbare as someone saying "Yo, Girlfriend!" or "What's up, Bro?" Yet somehow when Lahssan says it I know it comes from a treasure chest deep inside him where his English words are stored and selectively gifted.

—⁓—

Only a week earlier, I'd heard my brother utter the same word. While lounging on a metal chair in the Tuileries Gardens in Paris, my phone rang. I recognized the number right away, and since I hadn't spoken to my brother in a while, I answered.

"Hey Rickley!"

"Hey Sister, how's it going? I hope I'm not bothering you, but I have a few questions about Paris."

"That's *so* weird," I said into the phone. "I'm actually *in* Paris right now."

He feigned surprise, but we both knew it wasn't really so weird. As twins, we were used to such uncanny coincidences.

A favorite movie of ours when we were growing up in the '70s was *Escape to Witch Mountain,* in which twin brother and sister Tony and Tia move things without touching them and communicate with one another using only the power of their minds. As much as we wished we could speak telepathically during school or freak our mother out by rearranging the furniture from our fort in the backyard, it just wasn't our schtick. We did try once, holding hands over our Formica kitchen table, silently imploring our cereal bowls to whirl like dervishes, but we couldn't provoke even a ripple in the milk.

In school, friends often asked silly questions like, "Can you read your brother's mind?" or "If I punch you in the arm can he feel it?" I always said no, because it was the truth. At the time, I didn't understand that the curiosity behind these inquiries was the mysterious link twins are perceived to have. I never thought much of it since many siblings boast strong bonds, but in the back of my mind it made sense that twins would have more enigmatic ties. After all, we'd been given a nine-month head start on forming a relationship while sharing a space the size of a watermelon, then set out on parallel paths through childhood and adolescence to endure the same stages and phases at the same time. We not only share 50 percent of the same DNA and a birthday, but until we were about two we also shared a bedroom, our cribs pressed one against each wall where my mother says we'd peer at each other through the slats as we fell asleep, talking in our own unintelligible language. It wasn't until we were adults, and our individual identities matured, that our connection became more tangible.

Put us in a pool together, even now, and Rickley and I will face each other and clasp hands then duck under water and press the soles of our feet together. Our butts will eventually bump, and we'll somersault backward before surfacing as we laugh and gasp for breath. Neither of us remembers when, where or why this folly started. Though we never manifested the magic of our favorite movie, we did always seem to inherently know when to reach out to one another. Recently, I'd locked myself out of the car after dinner with a friend in Los Angeles. Instead of calling a taxi or a roadside service, which I'd normally do, I called my brother's cell phone. He was working late and driving home, and just happened to be just a few blocks from where I stood.

Now here was my brother, a sound effects editor from California, calling me to ask me about the subway stations in the French capital, where I just happened to be. I stood in the *métro*, holding my phone out as arriving and departing trains pushed and pulled air through the underground tube, their doors swishing open and thudding closed—then sent my brother the recording.

———

Lahssan had started calling me Sister the morning after I arrived in Fez. I was chatting with Sue, the *riad*'s manager, before setting out to explore the medina when Lahssan shouted from an interior balcony overlooking the courtyard.

"Sister, wait. I have something for you."

I nodded okay then asked Sue if "Sister" was perhaps a common term young men used to address solo female guests, or foreign women.

"Neither," Sue said. "In fact I've never heard him call anyone that."

My heart warmed and fluttered, much like the candles inside the lanterns shimmering in the entryway. I'd been drawn to Lahssan immediately, too. Not in a romantic sense, but in the peculiar way kindred spirits are when they feel something imperceptible is at play.

"Sister, take this map," said Lahssan when he finally reached me. "If you get lost, I help you."

I unfolded it and began to laugh. It was a map of the medina, the walled-in old city of Fez, whose depicted streets took on the form and usefulness of cooked spaghetti noodles dropped onto a piece of paper. He'd put a red circle on the map to mark the location of our *riad*.

"It's no problem," he said, interpreting my confused reaction.

Lahssan opened the front door and stepped into the sheltered lane that smelled of damp cement and forgotten daylight.

"You keep walking up," he said.

He pointed toward an invisible 'there.'

—⁓—

When I'd first seen the medina from a distance, approaching from outside the ancient walls in a taxi, it looked dehydrated; sun-roasted to a golden hue the color of parchment paper; inert. But once inside the keyhole gates Fez thrummed even in its most static state. Embroidered with a pantone palette of colors, sounds, smells, and heatless shadows stitched together by the people that live and work among its tangled threads, the medina turned, reshaped and sang in real time. Men sloshed clothing in plastic buckets overflowing with saffron and indigo dyes, flooding the cracks between cobbles with tinted streams. Arabic and French, the two main languages of the medina, picked at either ear as I explored the city's puckers and pleats. *"Balek! Balek!"* "Attention!" Watch out! I pressed myself against a wall as a worn and matted donkey loaded with goods clattered past on gawky legs.

Another day, an incessant clang and ting lured me to a crowded square where metal craftsmen thumped mallets against brass, plying it into lamps, mirrors, cauldrons and jewelry from sunrise to stardust. The arrhythmic din vibrated the fillings in my teeth and jiggled my eyeballs in their sockets.

Even armed with a map and a good sense of direction, I got lost between the walls and unmarked streets, which became a daily occurrence. At times I was so deep in the medina that only the slivers of blue between grey buildings and the hazy fingers of filtered sunlight through a latticed ceiling reminded me there was sky above. Every now and then I'd peek inside a cracked doorway or follow the tinkle of a fountain to a hidden courtyard with purple flowering vines climbing up balconies stacked like bookshelves. In one garden I found silence, a rare flower amid the medina's cacophonic bouquet. I daydreamed on a bench in the shade of a lemon tree whose branches drooped with yellow orbs. From inside a window above, peals of children's laughter broke the reverie. All I could see were their dresses and shirts dangling on a clothesline stretched between buildings, flapping against a sapphire sky.

The song "Eye of the Tiger" rolled toward me down another nameless lane. For an instant, the music carried me back to the summer of 1982 and Niagara Street in suburban

Los Angeles where my brother and I rode our bikes. We'd just seen the movie *Rocky III* and as we pedaled up and down the sidewalk, turning around in the driveway of our house, we sang the lyrics and boxed at the air in tune with the song's opening instrumental salvos. The modern tune seemed incongruous in the ancient medina, and I eventually found its source. It was literally a hole in the wall, as if a supersized Rocky Balboa himself had punched his giant fist through the stones. Inside, a boombox blared next to a thirty-something-year-old man who, beneath the light of a single bulb, called upon his nimble hands to maneuver a clacking wooden loom over colorful threads that would eventually transform into a scarf, a tablecloth, maybe a rug.

There were thousands of shops like this in the medina that, when shuttered, were nearly indistinguishable and easily absorbed into the human routine of disregard. Once opened, however, they bulged dirt to rafters with anything from sticky nougat candy, gold jewelry, and crockery to spices, oils, and pointy, leather *babouche* slippers in gumball colors sold by leathery-skinned vendors whose open palms waved me in. Bargaining was expected, but I was not good at it and paid way too many Moroccan *dirhams*, I was later told, for the *djellaba* I'd purchased.

"Sister, why didn't you tell me you were shopping, I would have gone with you," Lahssan said when I arrived back at the *riad*, a plastic bag in hand.

"It's okay. I don't mind going alone."

"No," said Lahssan, putting his hand on his heart. "It's my job to help you, Sister."

"*Shukran*," I said, putting my hand over my heart, too.

Lahssan really didn't need one more job.

A few days into my stay, Sue had told me Lahssan lived in a small room on the top floor of the *riad*, which explained why he was at work day and night, pouring tea, hauling luggage up and down the stairs, serving breakfast first thing each morning and dinner to guests who decided to dine in each night. Even with his manic schedule, Lahssan still found time to leave extra candles in my cubby-hole room one day, which I never asked for, though had found it too dark to read in bed. As I sipped coffee at a café one afternoon, I saw Lahssan pulling suitcases from a taxi. I waved but it was crowded and I guessed he didn't see me because he didn't wave back. I watched him until he disappeared behind a wall with luggage and guests in tow; his stroll by turns determined and carefree.

—⁓—

The sugar from the freshly poured mint tea sticks to my teeth and coats my tongue. Alone in the *riad's* central courtyard I hear the *muezzin's* tinny call to prayer pour in through the open ceiling. It's bellowed five times a day from the mosques and minarets that pierce the sky over the medina and it trickles down the blue and green Moorish tiles that encrust the *riad's* walls and floors. I let it finish, making a mental note to tell my brother Rickley about the evocative sound, then dash up to my room to grab a few things before heading out for the night.

On the way back down, I see Lahssan talking to Sue at the bottom of the stairs. Gone are his leather slippers and the maroon-colored tunic he was wearing earlier, and in their place a red and blue soccer jersey, flowing shorts, long socks, and sneakers. I sit down on the stairs so we are looking eye to eye and smile, happy to see this youthful side of Lahssan. I ask him what he's up to.

"Playing soccer with my brother," he says, a smile carving its way across his mocha-colored cheeks.

He looks like any American boy back home, like the neighborhood boys we used to play with across the street. In my head I see a picture of my brother in sports clothes just like Lahssan's. Sue interrupts my daydream.

"Did you know Lahssan has a twin who also works here in the medina?"

Goosebumps prick my skin. I rest my chin in my hands, my elbows on my knees.

"No, I didn't," I say.

Like a movie montage in my head, I see Lahssan at the taxi stand, at the *riad* pouring tea, near the café when I'd waved to him. No wonder he was everywhere, there were two of him. I feel the invisible tie between us tighten.

"This might surprise you," I say. "But I, too, am a twin. I also have a twin brother."

Lahssan smiles. His chestnut-colored eyes warm and he puts a hand over his heart.

"Sister, now we are four in our family."

Later that night, Lahssan is nowhere to be seen, and I take the narrow stairs to the roof of the *riad*. Looking over the medina, a tapestry of staggered flat-topped houses unfurl across Fez in all directions. Their roofs are playgrounds and laundry rooms for families living below, and gardens for satellite dishes that sprout like sunflowers. Fez has existed for more than 1,000 years and will likely exist for 1,000 more. As thoughts of my own impermanence chisel their way into the spaces between flesh and bone, I feel like a solitary stone in the history of this place; one that will eventually turn to dust and blow away.

I remember another question someone once asked me about twins.

"They come into the world together so I wonder if it is common for them to leave the world at the same time, too?"

I'd dismissed it as the stupidest thing I'd ever heard until a few months ago when I was having dinner with my brother and he told me he's always felt as if he'd never live beyond fifty years old—just three years away.

Hairs tingled the nape of my neck.

"That's *so* weird," I said. "I've always felt exactly the same way."

We both knew it wasn't so weird.

The methodic hymn of the mosques sounds again, drawing people from the obscured fissures of the medina, a reminder that what is essential, much like faith, is often invisible. Only a week earlier I'd thought the medina looked dehydrated and dormant. But I've found that in places, as within people, life often dwells in the darkness and awakens when we cast our light.

The immensity of all that remains unseen overwhelms me, so I do what I've climbed up here to do. I take out my phone and record the *muezzin*'s haunting summons so I can send it to my brother when he asks for it, which I know he will.

Interwoven

Gloria Wilson

"DO YOU WANT A RAG OR A rug?" the antique carpet dealer asked. That fall of 1973, Jerry and I, married but a month, quickly looked at each other, each wondering if we were about to invest or squander his parents' wedding gift of money.

The rug seemed huge, a striking, cobalt-blue sea with an ivory design inlay. We imagined its life in distant places and times: Ming dynasty, in the Forbidden City summer palace, on a wall in Istanbul, in a *riad* in Fez. How it got to a dealer on the Main Line of Philadelphia, who knew. The rug was worn, threadbare on the edges, evidence of repairs in the center. But our eyes focused on the intricacy of the design and the brilliance of the color. This rug had history. It had meaning. It had a long life, one that we could become part of and continue.

Did we want a rag or a rug? Of course we wanted a rug, we agreed. We wanted something as complex, intricate, and interconnected as our love. We realized even then, so early, that we might not have a long life together, that diabetes would have a brutal effect on Jerry's body and on our lives. But we wanted to be interwoven like the design on the rug, to patina and become deeper and richer with time, to become worn but not worn out. The rug fit onto our VW Beetle and into our Queens apartment.

It became part of us as we moved around Long Island. The rug filled the living room of our cottage on a hill in Centerport, and barely fit in our small house in the suburbs of Freeport. It was dwarfed by the enormity of the converted horse barn on an estate in Syosset, and was the centerpiece of our sun-filled country house in Huntington.

I gave the rug to a friend before I moved to my New York City apartment. So many decisions to make, what to bring, what to leave behind. What brought back too many memories, what would keep me entrenched in the past, what would make me slowly smile. I took the mission furniture that we both loved, I took the stained glass lamps that Jerry made, I took the many cards he wrote, inscribed with touching and poetic thoughts, but I didn't take the rug.

Did I feel that the rug was by now too worn and battered? Too reflective of the years filled with hospitals and pain and fragments of dreams?

I'm in Casablanca now, in the spring of 2014. My mind is twirling like the spinning of thread, as an endless supply of nomadic rugs unfurl, revealing bursts of natural dyes made from plants, insects and minerals, and displays of intricate warp and weft threads laced together forming complex geometric, freeform designs. Could the carpet dealer be telling me this rug was tribal? This rug woven simultaneously by two women with 200 knots per square inch? This rug reversible for summer and winter? This rug made from live sheep wool not wool discarded by the tanneries? This rug embroidered inside a tent with naturally dyed silk thread, completed before marriage as part of her dowry? Did he say with a needle made of camel bone?

"Look Look! This rug took fifteen months. Gaze at the subtle shades of teal with a hint of burgundy. How can you put a price on a carpet labored over for all that time? This rug represents the tree of life. Here, have some mint tea. Take off your shoes. Don't just see the beauty, feel the beauty. Ah, you have expensive taste."

Do you want a rag or a rug? Could it possibly be forty-one years ago that we heard that question? Ten years since Jerry died, never having realized his dream to explore Morocco? Here I am alone, deciding by myself, for myself.

I gasp at the beauty I see and feel.

Do I want a rag or a rug?

Time or the Sahara Wind

Marcia DeSanctis

IN MY FAVORITE PHOTOGRAPH from my first visit to Morocco, I appear as if on the floor of a canyon. Behind me is a cinematic backdrop: a towering pomegranate-red clay mountainside speckled with clusters of trees. I'm standing on a wide open restaurant terrace, wearing white Capri pants and a black tank top, sneakers with no socks. The wind blows my hair into chaos but one hand pushes the bangs off my face. In the corner, over my shoulder, there is a sliver of Matisse-blue sky. I am twenty-four years old.

I recall arriving at this place, wherever it was, to the staggering sight of the mountains opening up beyond the valley and then, my mother's voice. "I'm just out of words," she says as her narrow foot swings lightly out of the car into the sunshine. "Isn't it something?"

My mother documented that trip to Morocco as she did every-thing in her life. Perfectly. Painstakingly. With the observant eye of a woman who was born an artist, but in a time and place where it would never have occurred to her actually to declare herself one. Me stroking a carpet or chatting with a merchant at the *souk*, my sandaled foot in the stirrup of each camel I rode (there were, I'm afraid, more than one), every mimosa blossom that riffled beyond the hotel window—it was all preserved on film. Back at home, my mother's deft hands slipped the photo-graphs into albums, which were left untouched for decades like monuments whose purposes are overlooked or forgotten, and certainly taken for granted.

The photos seem to be brushed with a brownish glaze. Maybe it's the passage of time, but perhaps it was the grit from the *chergui*, the wind from the Sahara that blows west across the Atlas Mountains and through Marrakech, Meknès, Ouarzazat, carrying fine particles of rust-colored sand. It was ferocious that year, the fall of 1985. The dust hung dense but invisible, and may have left a film on the lens of my mother's camera, giving the snapshots a tawny cast that dimmed the brights of morning and churned the milkiness of the clouds.

The fine orange coating on my skin made it erupt with tiny hives upon arriving in Marrakech and some memories of the trip now seem as if they were filtered through a pleasant Benadryl haze. Even the novel I was reading poolside at the Hotel Mamounia—*The Mists of Avalon*—bears remnants of this dry desert wind. The paperback remains on my bookshelf, smudged with fingerprints the color of dried blood on pages stippled from pool water that dripped from my hair and dried in the heat. My mother photographed that, too. Her youngest daughter, asleep in her bikini, stretched out on a chaise under the prickly sun with a book resting on her stomach.

There are no photos of my mother from that trip. This is the fate of many mothers, of course, who are so busy capturing memories for the family archives that their existence is obscured behind the camera. But even if she is invisible, her presence is everywhere in the pages of these two albums, collections of moments she created, assembled and enshrined. In each picture, she is there, reflected in my own eyes that faced both her and her camera. Back then, on the green lenses of her sunglasses, I saw a moving pinprick that was me looking at her. Her arms, legs and face were browned, and her short hair tousled from the stifling wind that rolled across the terrace. She grasped the camera and when the shutter snapped, her engagement ring, and the other one with a row of tiny rubies, flashed white in the sun.

This is the version of my mother that passes through me in dreams. I want not to forget the image of her as she was, vitality intact. Thirty years have passed and today her mind is a vacant chamber, her voice often a profusion of babbles. Occasionally she can muster up decipherable language, but rarely context for the words that emerge. In Morocco, with her suntan and the skin still tight across her cheekbones, her eyes were almost-sapphire dark. Today, her hair is a tangle of white semi-waves that the staff at her home frequently grooms back into place. That, plus the pale skin on her face render her eyes a vibrant, almost pastel, blue. I have looked at them forever but only really notice them now. Her gaze is direct but tinged with opacity, and I cannot know what it sees.

Though she is alive her life is behind her. So I seek her out by studying photographs not of her, but of me. It is in this gathering of images, through the negative space she dominates completely and in every frame, that I understand, miss and grasp most urgently for the woman she once was.

I don't think my mother was searching for much when she first inhaled the sweet, orange-blossom air in Marrakech, but Morocco was where she found herself. It was a midlife bloom, the triumphant gift of the empty nest. My father, a Boston cardiologist, was asked to look after King Hassan II's heart and occasionally made a house call to Rabat, Casablanca, Marrakech—wherever the monarch was in residence at the time—with my mother always by his side. Of course, they traveled in style on these brief jaunts to North Africa, but that was the least of it. My mother was from humble New England stock, an academic wife and a far cry from a social climber. She was very pretty but plain, barely wore makeup and certainly never colored her gray-streaked hair. In Boston, it was undignified to make pains to turn back the clock. Maybe it was the suntan, or the sudden swoosh of plum lipstick, or the muscular legs, no longer suburban, that descended from her light summer dresses, but in Morocco she blossomed like a teenager into a beauty.

She deserved the extra-big seat on the plane, the little dopp kit with Hermès perfume, and once in Morocco, the official car and driver who ferried her to the *souks*, to other cities and across the streams and valleys of the countryside. In Boston, my father was known and beloved for his dedication to his patients, his medical school students and to medicine— to being a physician and healing—writ large. But his success had a price. He also worked eighteen-hour days, seven days a week, leaving my mother to raise four daughters essentially alone. I can't imagine her exhaustion when she packed me, the youngest, off to college. Sometimes I wish I had asked her how she celebrated that first night in an empty house. *If* she celebrated. Perhaps she wept, now that the second half of her life sprawled before her and there was no grand plan.

Like most women married in 1955 she had given up her own work to be a wife and mother. It's still not clear to me if it made her happy or if she ever stopped to consider what she was sacrificing, and if resentment simmered beneath her unadorned exterior. I don't know what my mother questioned, if she ever questioned anything. I never asked her that either. I knew she loved us and that was all.

After her first trip to Morocco, it was clear that the country filled the great gaps that had opened in her life. She lunched with friends. She devoured *tagines* swimming with candied lemon peel and tart black olives. She gazed up at the ramrod-straight palm trees crowned with sprays of leaves that burst like feather dusters. She reclined by the pool in the hard sunlight, savored the warm breeze that blew across her face at nightfall, and loved to divert for a spontaneous meal of fresh fish and chilled wine on the beach in Essouaria. She trod her sandals over the rich green tiles and past the bougainvillea that grew in dense thickets along ramparts. She marveled at the oversized crowns of roses, two feet high and two feet wide, that His Majesty left in my parents' hotel room on each visit. She was dazzled by the mottled ochre walls and the lyrical disarray in the *souks*.

She was delighted that she, that daughter of a quarryman, could visit the palace (or palaces . . . there was one in every city) of the king she was invited by, but her real exhilaration came from how effortlessly she could transpose herself onto this strange and beautiful place, and freely seek adventure there. Sometimes, she stayed on after my father's medical work was done, even for a few days—still attended to by minders from her royal hosts of course, but unscheduled and on her own. My mother was entirely and happily liberated for the first time in her life and hungry to explore the country where she felt embraced and at ease. Here, she was always my father's spouse, but more than just a doctor's wife. Morocco dictated the flowing words of her second chapter.

And she wanted to share this new passion with me. I am the youngest of four girls and though I'm not the favorite by any stretch, it often worked out that I was the lucky beneficiary of my mother's generosity. I was the last one at home, suddenly an only child, so during those two years after my next-oldest sister left, I cleaned up on travel. My parents took me along when they could: to London, to Greece, and elsewhere. Maybe also they felt guilty about all the hand-me-down clothes I had to wear, the incessant teasing, or the cropped haircut my mother, grown weary of three older girls in braids, inflicted on me. They certainly made it up to me. That year, in 1985, while I stewed over changes both professional and in love, I was invited to Morocco.

———*w*———

My mother and I explored while my father met with the medical team, but more often the three of us were together, in Marrakech or on the road. We drove to the Atlas Mountains, to Meknès and the great Roman ruins of Volubilis. Often there are others alongside me and my father in the photographs, strangers who were in my life too briefly to remember their names: Moroccan physicians, their wives perhaps, the driver who always joined us for lunch. But in almost every image in the album, I appear. Here I am standing behind my own bursting bouquet of roses— hundreds of red, yellow, pink blossoms—on the terrace of our hotel. I am wrapped in a white robe and my eyes are puffy. I had been crying and though we hadn't discussed it, my mother knew—how could she not? I had received a pleading telegram at the Mamounia from the man I had left for another and my face bore a rictus of anguish.

In another, I am standing in front of a massive carved doorway.

"Isn't it beautiful?" she asks as she takes a picture of me. She is impossibly slim, in tan trousers and a light blue blouse. She snaps on the lens cap and stuffs the camera into her canvas tote. She hoists a bottle of water and takes a gulp.

"Are you thirsty, honey?" she asks. "Do you need sunscreen?"

Sometimes she photographed me doing business with the basket-makers in the *souk*, or buying a round of bread to nibble on, or ordering a glass of tea packed with mint leaves at the hotel restaurant. I am beside a donkey and my hand grazes the saddle. I seem intent while loading film into my own camera, or a tad awkward with a troupe of dancing girls in long brocaded *caftans* swaying behind me. Shoulders bared, I am in a sarong that is wrapped around me like a dress, seated on a mosaic fountain. In the pool behind me float thousands of roses cut from the stems. I look annoyed.

"Mom, please. All you do is take pictures," I likely said to her. "Don't you have enough?"

"You look so pretty, honey," she would have said and then sat beside me on the tiled ledge, listening to the splash of water into the basin.

There are many shots of my father, the driver and me at a restaurant, sitting around a table with her chair empty after she jumped up to chronicle these moments, too. As I look at the album now, I imagine her seated the second before the snapshot, opening our bottle of Sidi Ali water, mothering me to smithereens, asking if I like the stewed pumpkin or the lamb couscous I'd ordered for lunch. I wish it was she who had turned to face the camera once in a while, but I am comforted with the assurance that when I smiled into the lens, I was really smiling at her.

She loved to take pictures when I wasn't looking, as I do now with my own children. She was fascinated by this living entity she gave life to, and the sight of me seemed to never bore or tire her. In one shot, I lean over to inhale the scent of a pile of oranges. She snapped me with my eyes closed on a bench in the Majorelle Gardens. She captured me time after time with my face tilted up to catch the sun. I appear entranced, as if in meditation, but I was only grabbing a moment to turn myself a deeper shade of brown.

My mother was always there.

My mother is always there.

I returned to Morocco many times, several with my parents. I went to weddings and New Year's parties, but they were more rushed affairs, never with the desultory pace of my first trip with them. Occasionally I flew down from Paris, where I was living, with the man I married. My parents returned countless times to Morocco until King Hassan II died in Rabat in 1999. They had seen everything by then and still had never seen enough. My mother always took pictures, of course, but it was only during that first, perfect visit that she documented me with such persistence, as if she suspected I'd reach for these photos as an anchor thirty years later. Those photographs are aging much slower than we are and in them, I feel not just the presence of the woman who loved me. More intensely, I sense a woman I knew, someone exactly my age now who was tackling her hard-earned freedom with wonder, openness, and a sense of abandon. She hurled herself upon the big, open landscape of Morocco and found her place in the world.

Twenty-five years passed since she had first landed in Casablanca, and she was well into her seventies when she realized she wouldn't return. In truth, these cross-ocean voyages were trying, even in first class. Even so, she mourned the end of her travels there with enough grief and nostalgia to make it clear that the sense of loss was for something more than just Morocco and maybe a decent couscous (something that never quite made its way to Boston).

Then came her decline. It was slow, but inevitable. These days, my mother's sweet little room at her Alzheimer's home is decorated with a few things, now relics, from the *souks* she roamed so freely. Over the years, she amassed a lot of stuff, most of all carpets that seemed to be delivered to my parents' home with stunning frequency, as if my mother could not resist another tactile remembrance of the place she loved and belonged. There is a small woven basket, a little silver tea pitcher with a long spout. On the wall is a framed menu from one of the king's New Year's parties, engraved with gold and royal-blue script, all in French. When I visit her there, I like to chat about her travels to Casablanca, Marrakech, or Fez, as if mention of them might dislodge a secret door to a clear, bright place.

"How many times did you go, about a hundred?" I ask.

"That first trip with you and Dad was one of the best times of my life. Remember how happy you were to show me the Jamaa el Fna?" I ask.

"There must have been a million roses in those bouquets at the Mamounia," I say.

"I hated the bones in pigeon pie," I say. "Didn't you?"

Last time I went to see her, I brought a photograph. It's impossible to know what an Alzheimer's patient is seeing, and least of all remembering. "My favorite picture of me ever is from Morocco," I say. "You took it."

I open my purse and remove an envelope, which contains the shot of me on that great open terrace, under a brilliant slice of sky with the clay slopes behind me. Like all the others from that year, the picture is tinged a slight rusty brown.

She looks at it. "Yes," she says.

"You can't see yourself, but you are there," I say.

She nods.

"You took this picture. You were wearing a grey flare skirt, a navy short-sleeved blouse and little blue flats that day."

She stares.

"In this picture, I am looking at you. You are younger and you are beautiful. You are my age, the age I am now. And you are looking at me," I say.

She stares.

"I am Marcia, your youngest daughter, and you showed me Morocco."

She tilts her head.

"Here," I say. "This is me, and I'm looking right at you."

She turns her face to me. Her hair is unruly, and though she is usually tidy, there are dribblings of soup on her sweater. She grasps my hand. Her grip is soft and her skin is smooth, her touch as soft as the drape of a filmy scarf.

"Except I have no idea where this is. Near Marrakech? I just don't remember," I laugh.

She fixates on the photo again.

"Do you know where this is?" I ask. "You know Morocco better than anyone."

She turns her face up to me and a smile unfolds like a handkerchief across her face. The gray creases brighten, her mouth unfreezes, her whole aspect alters in a millisecond from moribund to dewy and bright. Her eyes a shattering blue.

"Yes!" she shouts, startling me. She shakes her head vigorously as if to say, "Of course I do!" My mother takes the photograph from my hand, sets it on the table beside her and closes her eyes. Her lips are still turned upward in a smile, but within seconds her face is glazed with tears. I reach over her and take the photograph, slip it back into the envelope.

She grasps my hand again and squeezes gently. Her fingers graze mine with a light sound, soft as the rustle of mimosas on a warm night in Marrakech.

Change

I alone cannot change the world, but I can cast a stone across the waters to create many ripples.

—Mother Teresa

Writing is one of the most ancient forms of prayer. To write is to believe communication is possible, that other people are good, that you can awaken their generosity and their desire to do better.

—Fatima Mernissi, author of *Dreams of Trespass: Tales of a Harem Girlhood*

Common Ground in the Kasbah

James Michael Dorsey

THE CORNER TABLE ON THE patio of the Argana Café in the Marrakech Medina was the perfect place for me to sit each morning and watch the busiest public square in Africa come to life under a golden sunrise, that fall of 2002.

Rabat is the capitol of Morocco, and Marrakech is its heart, but the medina, its center, is an Arabic word that simply means "town," and it is the soul that beats the heart.

Marrakech is a Berber word that translates roughly to "Land of God." It was founded by the Almoravid dynasty in 1072 and was so powerful a city that until the 20ᵗʰ century all of Morocco was known as the Kingdom of Marrakech. The Jamaa El Fna Square, in the medina, is a churning cauldron of humanity that only stops long enough each night to catch its breath for the next day. Jamaa El Fna can be said to mean "gathering of trespassers."

At sunrise, merchants and vendors flow in like a slowly creeping tide; umbrellas and awnings sprouting like mushrooms. Snake charmers, rock stars of the square, claim their ground with cheap carpets on which they deposit numerous rubber snakes to give volume to the handful of living ones they actually possess. Next, they bring out puff adders with lips sewn shut, followed by cobras so tranquilized they cannot strike, while good ol' American-style de-fanged rattlesnakes round out the menagerie. Still, the presence of such exotic and normally lethal creatures draws a paying crowd. More than any other attraction it is the snake handlers in their pointy yellow shoes, playing their flutes while a supposedly mesmerized cobra sways to its melody that defines the medina in my mind.

Leashed monkeys are trained to take money (and occasionally cameras) from tourists, while red-suited water vendors in bright red hats hung with multi-colored dingle balls, costumes unchanged in centuries, offer brass cups of water, a tradition left from ancient caravan days. Jugglers and fire-breathers supply diversions for the pickpockets whose nimble fingers relieve distracted tourists of their wallets. *Galibayas* (long traditional robes) and *kufiyas* (flowing checkered cloths held in place by a black forehead band) outnumber baseball hats and sunglasses here. As I sip my chocolate coffee I notice a woman with henna-dyed hands looking my way through the slit of her *burka*, her stylish, high-heeled shoes clicking on the ancient ground while she sips a fruit smoothie through a straw under her veil.

By mid-morning it is a nonstop, no rules, sea of humanity, where anything can be had if you know the right person, and a few extra *dirham* might bring forth a hidden treasure from under a vendor table. If you don't have a connection, money takes its place. It is the romance of the kasbah meets Barnum & Bailey. People watching in Marrakech is interactive, as vendors, shoppers, and tourists are all swept along by the never-ending human tide.

So it was from my corner table each morning that I would nurse my coffee and jot notes for future stories. Ideas would come like fastballs as the endless parade of costumes, smells and personalities overloaded my senses. In the afternoons, I would take wide, meandering strolls through the maze of vendor's stalls, passing street musicians with their hat tassels twirling in time to their playing, and marveling at the endless colors and embroidery patterns that gave life to otherwise drab *burkas*. I followed my nose to burlap sacks full of saffron and turmeric offered by toothless old women smoking hand-rolled cigarettes. I avoided eye contact with the young boys decked out in hennaed eyes that spoke of unthinkable acts.

One could not help but be bowled over by the sheer spectrum of items: Endless rows of tables held watches that did not run, bowls of animal teeth, pirated CD's, decades-old cigarette packs, knockoff designer jewelry, and endless knick-knacks culled from endangered species. If you can dream it you can buy it in the medina, and so it was in this cornucopia of the bizarre that I spotted the train.

It was an ingenious little toy. A white-turbaned Osama Bin Laden sits on a skateboard on a circular red and blue plastic track no larger than a hand towel. Behind him, George W. Bush, clad in military fatigues and sitting astride a double-barreled gun, is pursuing him in an armored vehicle straight out of a Mad Max movie. Both figures are about an inch tall. George's "tank" holds a single double A battery that drives the tank and a magnet on each vehicle repels the other as Bush chases Bin Laden in a never-ending circle; the epitome of tourist kitsch imitating life. It was so tackily cool, so current, so . . . MARRAKECH! As soon as I saw it I knew I had to have it.

Now this was a year after 9/11, and much of the world was still leery of travel. By my reckoning, there were not that many westerners in the medina at that time and our presence did not go unnoticed. While on the road I try to maintain a low profile, but I am continually told that I "look American." I am large with a California accent, which usually gives me away. Perhaps that day it was my Frank Zappa T-shirt and wrap-around shades that made me conspicuous, but eyes turned my way when I walked by. Still, I was blindsided by how quickly my wonderful discovery segued into a bad B movie.

My first reaction at seeing the train was one of those nervous, split second laughs that come from deep inside of their own volition to embarrass us at inappropriate moments, like laughing at a traffic accident. It was more of a startled exclamation, and yet it was enough to stop the conversation of four vendors who were sharing a morning's cup of tea from a communal samovar, whose eyes turned as one in the direction of my audible *faux pas* and fixed me with a stare of utter contempt; a stare so vicious it carried as much physical weight as a slap. These were hard men, men of the desert used to settling disputes at the point of a knife and whose faces carried scars that showed it. I was on unsteady ground.

I picked up one of the pre-packaged trains and held it up with a polite smile to infer that I wanted to buy it. The smallest of the four men, his head wrapped in a dirty *kufiya*, with that perpetual look of always needing a shave, stepped forward to snatch the package from my hands, spitting out an Arabic invective along with his saliva. He was livid, glaring so intensely I could taste the hatred.

His message was clear; no infidel was going to buy his plastic Bin Laden.

With a polite nod I turned to walk away but the little man came after me, waving his arms and announcing my evil deed to all within earshot. My momentary lapse of cultural sensitivity began to snowball.

I have always tried to consider both sides of every issue, especially while on the road, and was quite aware that I was in a Berber, Muslim country, while my own homeland was actively fighting other Muslims, but, in my experience most people make a distinction between benign travelers and their warmongering governments. The bottom line was, I had done nothing intentionally wrong. I was simply a westerner and the toy train raised a touchy subject in that time and place. I should have tread more lightly.

The man continued to follow me, yelling and gesturing like an Italian traffic cop, and he was beginning to attract a crowd. I picked up my pace, hoping to lose him in the crush of humanity. I passed several other toy trains for sale but did not stop for any of them. It was time to get out of Dodge.

By now there were five or six curious onlookers joining the posse and the little agitator who was now on a roll, had them whipped into an anti-tourist, no-plastic-train-buying mob. They looked like giant chess pieces ready to do battle, lined up in their robes and turbans, some fingering curved daggers in their sashes, talking as much with their hands as their voices. It was a gathering of testosterone looking for trouble.

I turned a corner to lose myself in the maze of the *souk* but paused only a brief second to look behind me, and at the sight of the robed posse I broke into a cold sweat. I was now being hunted on the enemies' home ground. I could make out the word "American," floating about, and it did not sound flattering. I had become prey.

The adrenalin was pumping as I beat a hasty retreat, doubling back in alleys and ducking into small shops to see if the lynch mob was still on my trail. For a while, it seemed that I had lost them.

I turned into a hole-in-the-wall shop with heart racing and added the caffeine of another cup of coffee to think things through. After years of travel to remote places, even those where I might have expected hostility, this was the first time I had been confronted by it based solely on my nationality and it was unnerving.

My mind was sorting through all of this when I looked up to see a small man in a checkered *kufiya* staring at me through the café window, freezing me in a moment of fear. I did not recognize this fellow from the medina. He wore glasses and his robe was finely embroidered and that set him apart from the rest of my trackers. He was obviously zeroed in on me, or was I just paranoid? Wondering if I had been cornered by the mob I rose to find the back door when the little man broke into a lopsided smile and raised his palm for me to sit.

He walked into the coffee shop, shuffling his slippered feet like a young child who had been caught sneaking something, and pulled one of the packaged trains out from under his robe, placing it on the table in front of me with a shy grin.

When I managed to close my mouth, I fumbled for some bills but he held up his hands to say no. We had no common language but there really was no need. I could see the embarrassment in his eyes. His simple act was an apology for his countrymen's actions.

I don't think he could have followed me, so apparently he had simply wandered through the *souk* until he found me because he thought it the right thing to do. Emotions collided within me: guilt for my cultural insensitivity, fear of the crowd following me, and bewilderment at hostility being so suddenly replaced by kindness. This jumble of feelings was mixed with gratitude for the finest expression of humanity my travels had ever gifted me.

I offered him a chair and he asked the waiter for juice while I ordered a third coffee. For a moment we sat in silence, eyes locked in understanding, our unspoken words needing no translation. I can still remember his yellow, crooked-toothed smile that spread to his jaw and said more than any words could.

Since that day I have often reflected on that afternoon and the man who brought me the train. I think of him every time I look at it on the shelf in my garage. Every so often I set it up on my dining room table and watch the endless pursuit go round and round.

In April of 2011 a militant cell claiming a connection to Al Qaeda blew up the Argana Café, killing seventeen and wounding twenty-five. The same people who passed my table at the café and entered my notebook to give me this story fell victim on that terrible day. As I had sat there writing, I'd been unaware that the silent forces that would eventually launch the Arab Spring were in motion, beginning to sweep across North Africa and the Middle East like a tidal wave.

Now when I prepare for a journey my friends ask how I can travel when it is so dangerous, and I tell them that travel is necessary if we are ever to have a lasting peace. Only by continuing to meet new people in new places can we ever reach mutual understanding. Only by traveling can we attain the realization of how much more difficult it is to strike someone you know personally than it is to hate someone you know only from electronic sound bites.

That day, anyone who passed by the table deep in the Marrakech Medina and saw an American in a Frank Zappa

T-shirt sharing a drink with an Arab Muslim in a *kufiya* would not know that it was a simple child's toy that had brought us together, or that two thousand years of suspicion and mistrust were melting away over coffee and a juice.

What they would know is that one of us had to travel to get there, and the two of us had found common ground.

Doors Open in Morocco

Ann Dufaux

O NE EVENING IN THE SPRING of 2014, a group of us were
returning to our *riad* in Moulay Idriss when we heard chanting,
tambourines and *darbuka* (drum) beats. The room was crowded
with the people of the neighborhood, who invited us in. We
learned that the music, played by four men in white *djellabas*,
was part of a Sufi ritual, a Last Judgment Ceremonial, in which
it is believed the spirit rises from the deceased. Heads swayed
to the trance-like music.

I noticed two girls filming the event with their phones. The
older women wore traditional headscarves, but these two were
bare-headed. The taller one dashed back and forth, her auburn
ponytail swinging, and the smaller girl flashed dimples as she
snapped, saying, "Sorry, sorry!"

I wondered how the future of these girls would be different than what I understood current conditions for women in Morocco to be.

Before my trip, I had read that in parliament one woman brought up the question of equal representation and her voice had been drowned out by heckling men. I'd learned of a clause voted in parliament entitling rapists of under-aged women to avoid prison sentences by marrying their victims. The law was eventually repealed, due to widespread outrage after a fifteen-year-old country girl was forced to marry her attacker and committed suicide.

In Fez, I met a craftsman sitting in a passageway of the medina embroidering blue Berber motifs upon a pillowcase. I asked him why I seldom saw women working in shops, and he said, "Be not mistaken, 80 percent of the work is done in homes by women. We men only give the finishing touches." *Piecework with the lowest pay,* I thought.

I noticed, among the men crowded into a terrace café, two women from our group, who stood out with their flaming hair. The few Moroccan women I saw had their heads covered and were escorted by males.

Before leaving France, I'd met Khaddouj online through my daughter. Once a university French professor, she is now president of a 14,000 member microcredit association she set up in the region of Meknès in 1995, of whom 70 percent are women. Khaddouj called when I arrived in Fez and said she wanted to take me to an association meeting.

When she came to pick me up at my *riad*, I noticed that no scarf covered her hair and she wore sports shoes and pants.

We drove about an hour and circled the 25km wall ringing the city. Beyond the wall lay thousands of simple white slabs—characteristically turned towards Mecca—scattered over hillsides among eucalyptus trees, forming a peaceful landscape.

Meknès was founded in the 17th century by Sultan Moulay Ismael. We entered the city center through marble columns that had been moved by the Sultan from the nearby Roman city, Volubilis. We passed an impressive granary with multiple stone arches where wheat was once moved upon thousands of horses and donkeys.

We visited the Mausoleum of Moulay Ismael, the only mosque non-Muslims are allowed to visit in Morocco, and the vast underground jail into which rebellious slaves were once thrown.

We drove to a building on the outskirts of town with a large panel written in French, Arabic and Berber: ATTADAMOUNE, the Microcredit Solidarity Without Borders Association.

We were welcomed and ushered into a room where three women stood up, saying: *"Es salaam alaykum."* We hugged Moroccan-style, touching our heart with our right hand, then sat down at a table laden with olives, nuts and drink.

"We're here to celebrate International Women's Day. These three ladies have done remarkably well setting up small businesses thanks to microcredit loans," said Rhizlane the local manager, who was dressed in pants with a green headscarf.

Abdullah, the young administrator, told me he welcomed my questions, and the women began to tell their stories.

Years ago, Fatima, in her mid-sixties, had requested a loan to run a café, as she needed to become the breadwinner for a large family after her husband's stroke. Her first trial loan of 1000 *dirhams* had lasted four months, and helped her get started. Soon business expanded and her two adult sons became her partners. I wondered about her daughters, but she told me they had families to raise.

Khadija, the most elegant of the three, was wearing a yellow silk scarf and a black *kaftan* adorned with yellow lace and round cotton buttons. She was an independent seamstress, specializing in creating elegant *kaftans* with crocheted trimmings, and she showed us a few. Her business was growing, she said. She'd hired four other women full time.

The presentation by the matchmaker Naïla sent my imagination reeling. Her ruddy cheeks and engaging smile made me want to know her better. I'd heard of the importance of matchmaking in the Maghreb and wanted to know whether the job was still popular.

"Years ago I would have not only organized the wedding, but ensured that the match between bride and groom was right. This matchmaking tradition has been lost in towns and cities, but I have plenty to do making sure not a single element needed for the traditional wedding is missing."

I wondered whether brides wore Western-style gowns. "People like to stick to tradition, but the cost of making gowns is exorbitant, so I rent seven different styles of dresses typical of the seven Moroccan provinces."

Naïla has professional henna painters create delicate motifs on the bride's hands and feet the day before the wedding. She finds venues, orders food, drink and flower arrangements. She also rents silver and gold jewelry, and *Amaryas,* thrones, on which bride and groom, seated side by side, are carried high above their guests by four men who circle the hall, while women ululate joyfully.

We moved on to a larger room where about thirty women waited for the meeting to begin. Rizlane offered to translate as Abdullah spoke to the women. He explained that a loan is not to be used to buy a stove or refrigerator. "No matter how badly your family might need either, your loan is exclusively for the project stipulated in the contract." Most of the women are peasants and cannot open a bank account, so their transactions are done using cash.

Khaddouj spoke next. On the occasion of International Women's Day she brought up the question of domestic violence.

"When conflict arises, settle it with words. We must avoid becoming the victims of physical violence, no matter what."

One woman said, "When my husband beats me, and he sometimes does, I know it's because he cares for me."

Many protested. The oldest in the assembly, appearing to be in her seventies with a weather-beaten face, stooped over with her hand on her back, but made an effort to straighten. "My husband died many years ago. In my early years, I had my share of beatings whenever his boss shortchanged or exploited him. One day I'd had it. I told him: 'Don't you dare raise your hand and beat me or the children. You may have your woes but we can talk things over.' I've warned my sons, daughters and their spouses that I won't take any more of that. We need to talk, not beat people or be beaten." There was a moment of silence, and then applause.

Each member was offered a certificate, a silk rose, a wrapped present, and then the women filed out, their joyful cries echoed down the street.

On our way back to Fez, Khaddouj said, "We have a long way to go. In 2004, three fourths of women in rural Morocco were still illiterate. You've noticed how things are moving in the right direction. Women work hard and want a better life for their children and themselves. They're becoming empowered.'"

Later, I discovered that the literacy of Moroccan women has improved slightly thanks to new literacy programs, mostly attended by young people with means. Poor girls under the age of eighteen still have little education or hope for jobs, and aim only to marry, as more of them do each year.

As we left the meeting, I thought of how much Khaddouj and this association had accomplished. I remembered the two young girls I'd seen at the gathering in Moulay Idriss, and wondered what I could do as an outsider that would open up more opportunities for their futures.

The next year, I returned to Morocco, and visited Khaddouj in her home. "We missed March 8th, International Women's Day, didn't we?" I said.

"Yes, and you missed ATTADAMOUNE's 20th anniversary celebration. By the end of the year we should have an additional six thousand members."

We picked sprigs of mint from her balcony, put some water on to boil, and, as Khaddouj guided me in measuring spoonfuls of sugar and timing the steeping, I imagined myself back home making this tea in my Paris kitchen, telling my friends about the changes that were occurring here, about Fatima's café, Naïla's weddings, Khadijia's *kaftans*, and the stooped old woman's strength.

Most of all, I'd tell them about Khaddouj herself, who was, one push at a time, opening doors for women in Morocco.

Window to a Wider World

Suzanna Clarke

To build up a library is to create a life. It's never just a random collection of books.

—Carlos María Domínguez

STEPPING THROUGH A DOORWAY into a small square, I looked up the street. The clang of the metal door alerted a group of eight young children, who raced toward me, joyfully calling out, "It's open, it's open." They crowded around the entrance, jostling for access to what lay within.

Their enthusiasm wasn't for a new video game parlour, or a sweet shop, or a figure in an animal costume, but for that age-old form of knowledge transmission, escapism and entertainment—books. At that moment I realized the new Medina

Children's Library was going to be a success. The modest two-room space, with its grass-green carpet, colourful cushions and shelves with books containing hundreds of magical stories, had connected with the small people of the Fez Medina.

The project had begun two months earlier, when two friends and I hatched a plan to start a community library. The idea came from Cathy Bellafronto, who had seen the shop space vacant, looked at the kids hanging around her neighbourhood, and had a vision to create a place for children. There are none in the medina—not so much as a single playground for children to occupy their time outside of school hours.

The Fez Medina is a medieval city, comprising more than nine thousand narrow streets and alleys. There are no cars, only donkeys and foot traffic. With its myriad mosques, and thousands of artisans, it is considered the spiritual and cultural heart of Morocco. It boasts the world's first university in continual operation, Al Quaraouiyine, started in 859 by Fatima al-Fihri.

Yet in contemporary Morocco, illiteracy is widespread. The average level in 2012 was measured at 33 percent, while in cities illiteracy among women was an astonishing 47.6 percent compared to a male level of 25.3 percent. In the medina this figure is likely to be higher, because of poverty and shifting populations. A large number of wealthy families left Fez during the colonial era, when the French made Rabat their capital. Then there was an influx of families from the countryside into the medina, after an extended drought.

Around 27 percent of rural girls are in primary school, but just 7 percent of them make it to high school. This is often because of economic reasons, and also because they may need to travel long distances and are potentially vulnerable. I have met many women, including our housekeeper, Rachida, who can't read or write, as they were sent out to work at a young age or required to stay home to care for younger siblings.

Naturally those without the ability to read and write have severely limited job options. Most modern ways of making a living revolve around the written word, whether it is reading signs or contracts, paying invoices or working on a computer. The illiterate are also at the mercy of others to interpret their environment for them. Even artisans, who make their own products by hand, have a greater ability to control how that product is sold if they can participate in the sale.

Houses I have visited in the medina rarely have books beyond the Koran, and certainly none for children. Lots of children don't continue their education past primary school and are expected to become part of the family business.

Reading was such an integral part of my childhood that it is difficult for me to imagine a life without it. I grew up in Australia, where there were numerous small libraries scattered through the suburbs of every city. Fez had just one, in the Ville Nouvelle, which recently closed. It had a modest children's section.

"Let's do it," was my immediate response when Cathy shared her idea about starting the library. So she and I had pooled money, time and resources, and Kim Fritschi contributed her time and expertise.

In our previous lives, we had had high-powered jobs. Cathy had been the deputy director of the Millennium Challenge Corporation in Morocco, an American foreign aid agency, and now runs a boutique hotel, Riad Laaroussa; Kim had managed a large legal firm in New York, and had her own business in Portland. I had been an Arts Editor, journalist and photographer on an Australian daily newspaper; and an author, and now also have an accommodation business in France. So, in typical Western fashion the three of us had meetings, made time-lines and lists, and dealt efficiently with the practical aspects. We set up a non-profit association, and invited a number of local Fez people to be in it. We knew that for the library to be successful, community involvement was essential.

But we had no idea if a library would actually appeal to the children of the medina. Speaking to locals, we discovered they were hazy on what a library actually did, and thought we were going to either sell books or offer tuition to their children.

Some middle-class Moroccan students I spoke to at the American Language Center in the Ville Nouvelle, a couple of kilometers from the medina, doubted the library would be used. Most of them rarely visited the medina, which they regarded as a lower class area, but they had definite opinions about the people who lived there. "Children in the medina don't read," they told me. "And their parents won't encourage them, because they just want them to go to work as soon as possible." They commented that smart-phones were all children aspired to, and that books were old-fashioned. But many among them were supportive of the concept and donated a significant number of second-hand children's books to the library.

How very wrong those doubters were. On the first day the Medina Children's Library opened, with no fanfare and without even a sign to announce its presence, more than twenty children came through the doors and raced towards the books, which were in Arabic, French and English. "This is the first time I have been in a library," said Aisa, aged ten. "Everything is beautiful—the room, the books and the stories."

Over the previous six weeks, the locals had completed the renovations, the books had arrived, and word had clearly got around.

The following day there were thirty children in the library, and the day after that I got a worried phone call from Kim, who was there with our newly appointed librarian, Safae. "There are more than thirty children here again, and a crowd around the door trying to get in," she said. I could hear the cacophony of excited children in the background, and the tension in Kim's voice. She said that the situation was unruly, and on the way to getting out of control.

At an emergency meeting the following day, we decided to limit access to only ten children at a time, for hour-long sessions, with a few more allowed in for story readings. And we appointed a guardian, a kindly older man, to control the door.

Cathy had gone to France shortly after our "soft opening," believing that just a few children and their parents would venture into the new library, and numbers would build slowly.

In the days before we opened, we said we would be pleased if we had eighty visits during the first month. In reality, there were more than seven hundred.

None of us anticipated the enthusiasm with which the library would be received. Children would line up at the doorway, long before it was open, slip off their shoes and rush to the shelves with excitement when they were finally admitted. Sitting on the cushions, they eagerly flipped through book pages. It was like watching hungry people devour a meal. They were completely absorbed in the books; often sharing discoveries they made in the pages with the children sitting nearest them.

I asked seven-year-old Lamiae why she chose to come to the library almost every day. "I feel like I am entering a palace of beautiful stories," she said. "When I am reading a book, I am happy because I feel like I am part of the story."

Wafae, aged nine, said "Before the library was here, I only used to play in the street with my friends." And little Kawtar, just five years old, added, "I come to the library because I want to read more stories. They stay with me always."

"The library is a novelty," we reasoned. "The numbers will drop off after a couple of weeks." But they didn't. They grew. We now have a system of issuing tickets for future sessions, so children don't have to wait around outside in the cold. Tickets are being allocated for sessions up to a week in advance.

The subjects of the books range from traditional Arab tales, like those from *One Thousand and One Nights*, to beautifully illustrated picture books, to Sci-Fi, science and history books, to European classics translated into Arabic. Some books have both Arabic and French or English text.

Until now, children have been reading the books there in the library. Now they have been catalogued, and we will begin lending books out. The children have been waiting impatiently for this. They can take one book for up to two weeks, by paying an annual subscription fee of 20 *dirhams*, (about 2 euros).

One of the best-loved aspects of the Children's Library is the volunteer story reading program, which is held daily and twice a day on weekends. Morocco is traditionally an oral culture, and children are used to being told stories by their grandparents and other older people. So having readers bring the books to life is a natural extension of this, and encourages them to discover the stories contained in the books for themselves.

One of the favourite readers is Aicha, who reads on Sunday afternoons. The children make a circle around her, and she begins by reading the classical Arabic softly, so they are forced to be quiet and still and listen. Then she becomes increasingly animated as she takes on the roles of the characters; her face that of an actress who knows she has the full attention of her audience.

While I don't understand much of the Arabic, I enjoy watching the faces of the children: at some points they smile, at others they look incredulous at the turn of events as the tale unfolds. Occasionally Aicha asks a question, and a dozen eager hands shoot up. Towards the end, they pass the book around and read a few lines. Often they stumble, and are encouraged by others.

One story Aicha read was about the importance of co-operation and trust. A little boy of about three years old piped up. "Except if they are going to cut your pee-pee," he said. The other children and Aicha fell about with laughter. The boy had recently been circumcised, and felt he had good reason to be suspicious.

Sitting with the children, sharing their enjoyment and listening to their laughter, I felt humbled and proud at the same time; suffused by the warm glow of happiness.

One day an Italian artist and designer ventured into the library, and offered his services. Carmelo Tedeschi had a studio in Fez, and along with other artisans created art objects that he sold in Europe. He had an idea for a project with the children, based on *The Little Prince*, by Antoine de Saint-Exupéry.

So on a Saturday morning, Carmelo brought art materials to the library, and he and the children made simple stars out of sponges, dipping them in yellow paint. "What is so different with these children from others I have worked with in Europe is the way they are used to making things with their hands. And the way they work happily with each other," he said.

The stars are now hanging from the ceiling of the library, by fishing line, which is almost invisible, so it looks like they are suspended by magic.

"All grown-ups were once children. . . . but only few of them remember it," wrote Antoine de Saint-Exupéry. I hope the library has reminded a few people about what it means to be a child; to be alive and curious.

Last weekend the Medina Children's Library was officially opened. We invited various officials and media organisations, but it was mostly the locals who came, keen to peek into what they had seen as a children's space. Several parents approached Cathy and me to say, "Thank you for what you are doing for our children. This is making a real difference to them."

While it was gratifying to hear that, this project has a great deal more potential. We would like to establish a cultural centre in the medina. At its heart would be a library for children and teenagers, plus workshops in art, theatre and music. A biennial Children's Festival could be part of the mix.

We have been approached by adults, both Moroccan and overseas-born, with skills in the arts that they would like to share. We know the children love being involved in anything creative. The next step is to source the funds to make the new Medina Children's Cultural Centre a reality.

When you come to Fez, please visit the Medina Children's Library. One need only see the animated faces and hands of the story readers; look at how absorbed the children are as they listen, then wave their hands in the air, desperate to share their knowledge. And, in the quiet times, watch the young faces as they delve into other worlds, other times, other places, far from the narrow streets of the mediaeval city they call home, and see how one small library can make a difference. Envision how a larger space could offer many more children the opportunity to create memories of art, music and books—nurturing curiosity in ways that will stay with them always.

Editor's Note: A percentage of the proceeds from this book will go to The Medina Children's Library. For more information, go to www.medinachildrenslibrary.org.

Cuisine

The (camel) burgers are by far The Clock's best-seller, so much
so that Mike spends much of his time trawling the bazaars in
search of fresh camel meat and the other ingredients needed for
his secret recipe. But his café is about much more than slaking
hunger pains. He feels a responsibility to highlight a little
of the heritage for which Fez is so renowned. Each evening,
after tucking into their burgers, visitors are invited to learn
from Moroccan experts. There are regular lessons in the art of
calligraphy, music and dance, and talks on local culture.

—Tahir Shah, "It's a Kind of Magic," *The Guardian*

Interview with Mike Richardson

Sabrina Crawford

When was the first time you came to Morocco and what impressed you about this place?

I first traveled to Marrakech and Essouira about eleven years ago. When I discovered through a mate that I was able to purchase an extraordinary medieval house in Fez for the same price as a parking space in London, I booked a flight immediately.

What I remember most is the incredible energy that pulses at the heart of Fez. My senses were heightened and my ingrained perceptions regarding the world were challenged.

What was it about Fez that made you feel this was the place for you and for Café Clock?

Café Clock came into being after having spent nine months searching for a property in Fez. I met many different people, local and international, who expressed the need for a buzzy, inclusive environment. As I had been working for many years in fashionable London establishments, I was sure I could pull it off. The opportunity to work alongside the amazing talents that thrive in Fez gave me the confidence and support I needed.

What did you hope and dream Café Clock would be? Remind us just a little about your background—where did you train and work before coming to Morocco?

The original idea was to depart from the tried and tested restaurant establishments in the medina. Until the opening of Café Clock there were only simple street cafés (generally the domain of men) and flashy Riad restaurants (for tourists). I was determined to have a fun, inclusive place where tables were close together and live local music could be played. The medina was crying out for a place for all to mix and have dialogue regardless of whether they were visitors or locals.

As a team we want to give access to the wonderful culture that exists, championing the creative spirit of my new adoptive home.

I have been a maître d'hôtel of some iconic London restaurants, such as The Ivy, Soho House and The Wolseley.

What inspires you in Moroccan cuisine and how do you come up with your amazing recipes?

The recipes come from a desire to create a modern Moroccan café menu. The produce, flavours and spicing are grounded in traditional cuisine but with a more universal appeal. Tariq, my first Head Chef, rejigged age-old recipes which he learnt from his grandmother. Tara Stevens, the food and travel writer, helped to define our menu through her enormous knowledge. She went on to write our lovely cookbook, *The Clock Book.*

What still surprises and inspires you about Morocco itself and life there, after all this time? What do you love most about living in Fez and Moulay Idriss?

I am constantly surprised by the depth of hospitality shown to me, and am therefore inspired to encourage this within Café Clock.

Now, in Fez, my brain remains active due to the constant barrage of stimuli, whereas my existence before my move here was much more by rote: eat, commute, work, sleep.

Moulay Idriss remains a refuge for me. A place that makes my heart sing. Living constantly in the medina of Fez can be too consuming due to its impressive but claustrophobic geography. In Moulay Idriss at Scorpion House the light, calm and sheer beauty of the views always reignites and refreshes me.

How many years have you lived in Morocco, and how long has Café Clock in Fez been open?

I have been living here for nearly nine years, and in October, Café Clock will have been open for eight years.

You've really created more than a café—it's a creative and culinary hub. What are some of your favorite memories and events?

My favourite memory was the Abbasiya. An Abbasiya is a party held by a new business where you invite all those who have been involved (builders, plumbers, chefs, etc) and the neighbours.

My job was to serve the vast platters of preserved lemon chicken and couscous. Prior to the arrival of our guests (men at lunch, women and kids in the evening) we had to offer a sacrifice to cleanse the building and bestow it with *Baraka*. We chose a chicken as I was squeamish about slaughtering a sheep (after eight years, thankfully, that squeamishness has gone). The event was terrific with the whole neighbourhood being welcomed with a blast of traditional long horns (*nfeh*) before tucking into the platters of food. The evening came alive with dancing and laughter.

What do you still love about running Café Clock? And what inspired you to open a new Café Clock in Marrakech?

I love that we are a stage. We regularly get young locals asking to play music, tell stories, create a TEDx event or start a poetry slam. . . . where else would this happen? It's exciting to be at the forefront of cultural revival and celebration. Marrakech came about as I became aware that although that scene is much more developed, there was still no place that enabled access to this amazing culture. Also I am working with a very talented crew who need to develop their skills and so a second venue allowed that to happen.

What are your hopes and dreams for Café Clock in the future?

Ultimately myself and the team would love Café Clock to grow beyond Fez and Marrakech. I am regularly asked why we do not open in Rabat or Casablanca. . . . I just hope we continue to have the energy needed to open more cross-cultural environments in this astounding Kingdom of Morocco.

Camel Burger Recipe

(Serves 4)

THE CAMEL BURGER HAS been a bestseller since day one, especially since the butcher revealed his secret ingredient: dried rose petals from the Dades Valley, that turns the patties into a powerful aphrodisiac. All who eat it, he told me, would be touched by love. Of course, if your local butcher can't get their hands on a juicy piece of camel steak, you could always substitute beef.

> 1 kg camel meat, minced
> 1 tbsp camel hump, or butter
> 4 tbsp red onions, chopped
> 6 garlic cloves, crushed
> 2 tbsp coriander, chopped
> 2 tbsp parsley, chopped

2 tbsp mint, chopped

2 tbsp dried rose petals

2 tsp ground cumin

1 tsp cloves, crushed

juice of lemon

salt and pepper

1. Put the lot through a food processor on pulse (don't make it too mushy), knead together and shape into 4 patties, cover and chill well before cooking (it helps the meat to bind together).

2. Fry on a dry pan or skillet for 4 minutes either side or to your preferred level of doneness

3. Serve on a toasted sesame bun with Taza ketchup and all the trimmings: a slice of cheese added to the patty just before the end of cooking time, slices of tomato and onion rings.

5-6 ripe tomatoes, roughly chopped

4 tsp ground cinnamon

4 tsp honey

olive oil

salt and pepper

Taza ketchup

1. Blend the tomatoes in a processor until fairly smooth then gently sauté in a little olive oil for 5 minutes

2. Add the cinnamon and sugar, season and simmer until the sauce is thick and glossy (about 10 minutes)

That Time Writer Michael Chabon Packed His Family Into a Minivan With a Stranger in Morocco

Michael Chabon

WE WERE HEADING DOWN to Fez from blue Chefchaouen and making decent time when our driver left the autoroute for a stretch of doubtful road. A modest sign pointed, in French and Arabic, to some unknown town.

I considered asking Rida, our minivan driver, about the reason for the change of route. I worked out the sentence in French in my head. But then I let it pass. Rida was a professional, and it was his country. In any case, I knew from long experience of travel in foreign countries and tongues that explanations, like dreams, only make sense while they're happening. Answers I thought I had understood perfectly when I heard them in French fell apart as readily as dreams when I translated them for my wife. At that moment I felt that I would rather not know the reason for the detour than know that I didn't know it.

Nothing moves me more profoundly, I hasten to add, than discovering the extent of my own ignorance. That is why I travel—by nature I'm a homebody—but sometimes it can be hard. Some days you get tired of decoding, of interpreting, of working to understand, of constantly orienting yourself, or, to put it another way, of being constantly lost.

"Why did you turn off the road?" my wife asked.

I looked back at Ayelet. She had a child on either side of her—"the Bigs," Sophie and Zeke, aged twenty and seventeen. In the back row were "the Littles," Rosie and Abe, thirteen and eleven. The boys had their headphones on, and the landscape unspooled past them to a hip-hop soundtrack; Action Bronson and Flatbush Zombies among the olive groves.

"Better to go this way today," Rida said. He seemed inclined to leave it at that.

"Is this the way to Volubilis?" Ayelet asked.

"No," Rida said, "the way to Zegota." Rida was handsome and soft-spoken. As with many men who have soft voices and serious eyes, it was hard to tell if he was f*#%ing with you. I thought I saw a smile gathering momentarily on his face, but it went away. "After Zegota, Volubilis."

"Zegota," Ayelet repeated, checking with me to see if I'd heard of it. I shook my head.

"Can we get lunch there?" Rosie asked.

"Not couscous," Abe said.

We all jumped on Abe for being so rude as to disparage Rida's national dish, but we were a bunch of dirty hypocrites. Everyone was sick to death of couscous. Moroccan cuisine is delicious and comforting, but it lacks fire and, above all, breadth. The spicy *harissa* I had enjoyed with my couscous in Belleville and the Goutte d'Or in Paris turned out to be a Tunisian thing; in Morocco you had to ask for it, catching your hosts off-guard, at times causing mild consternation. At nearly every meal in Morocco, the tourist is presented with subtle variations on four main courses: meat and/or vegetable couscous, meat and/or vegetable *tagine*, meat or fish skewers, and *b'steeya*, a savory-sweet pie of pigeon or chicken. Before arriving and during the first few days, the prospect of endless couscous and *b'steeya* had seemed heavenly. But ten days out from California, I found myself tormented by taqueria longings.

"Not couscous," Rida said. Now he smiled outright.

The country here was flat and, like so much of Morocco, under heavy cultivation with olives. In the clear late-December light, the silver leaves of the olive trees gave the day a wintry glint. Spreading plants with lush leaves grew among the endless ranks of *oliviers*. Rida said these were tobacco plants.

"Before, they grow the hashish here," he said. "Very good hashish. The best."

I saw that he expected this American whom fate had placed in the front seat of his employer's second-best minivan, dressed in a knitted wool *taqiyah*, or skullcap, and a hooded *djellaba* over an *Illmatic* T-shirt, to take an interest in the subject of hashish.

"Interesting," I said, trying to sound uninterested.

"Yes, but it is finished. The government says it will be better to grow the tobacco."

From a public health perspective, the underlying premise of this policy struck me as grievously flawed, but there was nothing much Rida or I could do about it. So I let it pass.

The road began to ascend, then turned abruptly horrible. At one point as we drove across a culvert, I looked down and saw that between the edge of the roadbed and the right-hand guard rail there were two feet of empty air.

The journey from Chefchaouen to Fez had seemed, on my phone, a fairly straightforward business, even with a minor detour to see what remained of Volubilis, the former capital city of the Roman province of Mauritania. So what were we even doing on this ex-road? Who was this man whom we had entrusted with our lives, knowing nothing about his temperament, intelligence, psychological history, or driving record?

"So, Zegota," I said.

"Zegota," Rida agreed. "No couscous."

I sank a little deeper into my *djellaba*. I'd just bought it in Chefchaouen's medina, but it was already beloved. It was a winter *djellaba*, woven of camel and sheep wool, patterned with vertical stripes of cream and coffee brown, and with a pointed hood that gives the wearer a wizardly air. When I wore it—though this was not my intention—I made a spectacle of myself.

Seeing an American dad walking with his American family in a fine Chefchaouen *djellaba* seemed to put a smile on people's faces. It might be a puzzled or a mocking smile, but even these were tinged with delight. Everywhere my *djellaba* and I went in Morocco—and I went everywhere in my *djellaba* and, to this day in wintertime Berkeley, wear it every night to walk the dog—I was followed by cries of "Nice *djellaba*!" and "Hi, Berber Man!"

After a bumpy hour, we neared the crest of a ridge. A string of villages ran along its top for ten or fifteen miles. The road was intermittently thronged with groups of children in school uniforms headed home for lunch. In the first town, the schoolchildren shouted and waved and peered into our car eagerly, as though prepared to be astonished by the identity of its occupants. Some little joker even pounded on my door. I jumped and looked at Rida. He was grinning.

"It's like they think we're famous or something," Rosie said.

The next village was indistinguishable from the first, but here, for some reason, we barely drew a glance from the school-children. It was as if all the relevant data on us had been gathered by the first group and transmitted to the second by no visible means. Word simply seemed to have spread: six Americans; Brad Pitt or Malia Obama not among them. Somehow, in the midst of our own lostness and ignorance, we found ourselves abruptly *known*.

That kind of thing happened to us all the time in Morocco. If we stiffed a kid at the far end of the medina for "helping" us find the way to a square that we already knew how to get to, a kid over in our end of town would seem to have heard about it and try to collect. When Abe felt sick on a hike in the foothills of the Atlas mountains, a muleteer appeared, seemingly out of nowhere, and set Abe onto his ready-saddled mule so we could carry on.

Rida eased the minivan around a hairpin bend and slowed down as we came alongside a low cinder block structure with a corrugated metal roof, open on one long side. It was divided by more cinder blocks into four deep, wide bays. It looked like the loading dock for a warehouse that had never been finished and was now home to squatters. Dark smoke boiled up from the center of the building.

To our surprise, Rida pulled into a sandy patch in front. Men in *djellabas*, tracksuits, and sweaters and jeans passed into and out of the shadows that filled the bays. On the concrete apron, a man with a poker was jabbing at half a bisected steel drum and unraveling long gray skeins of smoke into the blue sky. Behind him, a red curtain of carcasses—lamb and cow—dangled from steel hooks.

"Meat," said Rida. "Tell him what you want and the butcher will cook it for you."

We pointed vaguely at anything that did not still have a face or testicles attached, and fled. There was also a *tagine* on offer, chicken with peppers, and I ordered one of those, out of confusion and panic more than any desire to eat more *tagine*. On the far side of the butcher shop there was a dining area with a few picnic benches, and beyond that a vague space, empty but for some carcass-red rugs and three middle-aged men with beards and expressions of dignified boredom, sitting on bentwood chairs. I went over to see what kind of fare they had on offer and they stared at me the way you might stare at a wasp as it approached your Eskimo Pie.

"That is a mosque," Rida said, pulling me gently back to the dining area.

At that moment the butcher went past, carrying a large steel basket full of ground meat on skewers, and for the first time I understood that he did not plan on feeding us an entire limb or organ, freshly hacked. You made your choice of meat and it was ground, on the spot, and mixed with the owner's proprietary blend of spices, a formula he genially refused to divulge through an interpreter. The meat and its mysterious flavorings were rolled into flattened tubes along flat skewers like steel fence pickets, then caged in the basket so that they could be turned easily on the grill without falling apart.

I have eaten good food in unprepossessing locales, but I doubt the disparity between the crude, shabby atmosphere of that nameless cement-block dispensary of protein and redemption and the quality of the lunch laid on by the butcher of Zegota will ever be matched. When it arrived, the *kefta* was easily the best we ate during our two weeks in Morocco— and we ate a lot of *kefta*. The *tagine* arrived sizzling in its Munchkin-hat clay oven, the long, green peppers delivering a welcome and overdue burn. The ubiquitous mint tea was neither oversweetened nor bitter. The day was bright and cool, and after the meal we lingered a moment on that gritty concrete terrace, six Jews sitting in the sunshine between a mosque and a shambles, grooving on the mingled aftertastes of sugar and mint and barbecue and chiles, as happy, collectively, as we had been in Morocco or might ever be again in our lives.

"I don't get this place," Abe said, mopping the meat juices from his plastic plate with a hunk of *khoubz*, or flatbread.

I told him I knew what he meant. I thought about asking Rida if this unlikely meal was the reason he had taken such a long detour, if our growing discontent with the limited fare had somehow been guessed at and communicated—if, somehow, like the boy panhandler and the muleteer and the blasé school-children, Rida had *known* that this was what we needed. But I decided to just let it pass.

Quest

I rarely let the word "No" escape
From my mouth
Because it is so plain to my soul
That God has shouted "Yes! Yes! Yes!"
To every luminous movement in existence.

—Hafiz, "Every Movement"

Threads

Darrin DuFord

THE SIMPLICITY OF THE room struck me as borderline comical—concrete walls, King Hassan II in a snappy lounge suit watching me from a framed portrait, and a desk topped with only a typewriter and an ashtray blooming with butts. I was at the Fez police station, facing a detective whose cigarette ashed on the typewriter keys with each question he posed from the corner of his mouth.

I'll assume that most visitors to Fez end up exploring the maze of the city's 1,200-year-old medina, as opposed to the building where I currently found myself. I'd visited the medina too. And that choice led me here, into a brittle, wooden seat while Nora, the manager of my hotel, sat next to me and patiently translated questions from French to English.

The day before, I had been attacked by a young hustler on the street outside my hotel. On a previous day, I'd refused his alleged tour guide services and instead had paid another guide, one with a license, for a tour of the medina. The teenager just couldn't handle rejection, so he found my hotel and stalked the entrance. He had kicked my ankle after I'd turned away from him, while he scowled in perfect English, one of four languages he had used in his pitch.

In travelers' accounts both written and verbal, Morocco's fleet of ornery hustlers is almost as famous as the narrow covered passageways of Fez's medina. But such stories rarely end in violence. I knew it would be easy to allow the incident that brought me to this police station to commandeer my impressions and derail my desires. I had come to Morocco in hopes of gaining an understanding of the day-to-day rhythm of this country shaped by the influence of continent-crossing empires, of a monarch with a penchant for jet skiing, of past colonial overlords and the croissant recipes they left behind.

Yet instead of feeling thwarted, I began to feel as if the teenager had unwittingly gifted me an opportunity. The room, with an ambience rivaling that of a storage closet, seemed far from the scenes I'd been experiencing, the scenes I'd thought would prove the most defining—the chaotic crush of the medina, with its stacked nougat bricks, single-file foot traffic, and inexhaustible donkey droppings; its mingling scents of enchanting curry and putrid rivers; its beautiful children poking at my buttocks to try to find my wallet. Yet I began to find the sparseness of the detective's office, lightly peppered with the percussive clicking of keys, equally as defining.

I glanced at the soft curves of the man's face and his placid, brown eyes, fixed upon the paper, which imparted the impression that he was tapping out a letter to a friend instead of a police report. I realized the significance of the moment, because nothing speaks of day-to-day rhythm like paperwork taken in stride in front of a mechanical typewriter, all under the vigilant stare of the country's recently deceased monarch.

The gentleness of the moment almost hid the underlying cause of the meeting. The police wanted the teenager for two offenses: assault and guiding without a license, the combination of which could result in jail time owing to Morocco's recent campaign to crack down on illegal guides and reduce the harassment of visitors. The imprisonment of an unlicensed entrepreneur, even one with an unsavory sales pitch and questionable experience, seemed somewhat heavy-handed, but I remembered that Morocco is also a country where the CIA was found to have brought suspected terrorists for enhanced interrogation techniques that are illegal on U.S. soil.

"The police will start making a sweep of the area," Nora said.

The day before my trip to the police station, I had watched the cook impale a plastic lid with the tip of a metal poker, glowing red with heat, hissing on contact. While the lid of the paprika-filled shaker jar was still exhaling tiny rings of smoke, he placed it on the picnic table I shared with five men as we dipped pieces of wood-fired half-moon bread loaves into bowls of lamb *harira*, a thick soup. The harira clung confidently to the bread that served as an edible spoon—in fact, the only utensil available.

As I sat at the table, I replayed shards of the encounter with the young hustler in my mind in an attempt to process it: Alami wearing the same loose-fitting *djellaba* and the same stare—monomaniacal, desperate—as he had the day before; a spectacle of curses; frustration boiling; shouts of "You think I am just a stupid person?" and "Do you know how we work here?"; a sharp kick to the back of my ankle, leaving what would ripen into a fist-sized bruise. After I'd stepped inside the hotel, the receptionist insisting on calling the police; by the time he began making the call, Alami was gone.

The bruise was annoying but superficial. The soup was stunningly flavorful—a smooth jumble of meat and sweetness and lingering spice.

I'd decided to walk off the attack, and Fez had apparently rewarded my decision. While wandering around the Ville Nouvelle, the French-designed quarter of the city awash in traffic circles and wide boulevards and plazas, I had found this open-fronted restaurant by sight alone, since it bore no signage and no menu, only a crowd of men (conspicuously absent: women) silently pushing soup-drenched bread into their mouths.

Despite my limited French and my obvious foreignness, the patrons and the countermen offered me the same courtesies as to everyone else. The men at the end of table passed down bread to the rest, a half-moon for each of us. For a moment, I was just another hungry patron.

I thanked the young counterman in both French and Arabic for the five-*dirham* lunch—50 cents for a bowl of soup, a corpulent chunk of bread, and two mint teas. I received a warm, smiling *shukran* in return.

Hostile, then welcoming. I was beginning to realize that in Morocco they are part of the same tapestry.

—〰—

It was the tiny, unannounced actions and details that were revealing this tapestry's threads, as if the exquisitely tiled archways and minarets served as clever concealment. After I left Fez by bus and followed the foothills of the rippling Middle Atlas Mountains to the city of Meknès, a taxi took me to Volubilis, the ruins of one of the westernmost outposts of the Roman Empire. I don't remember much about the ruins, aside from the bird nests atop some of the few standing columns. But I still remember Ahmed, the cab driver, and the blue, bubbly, whimsical fish pattern on the clear vinyl of an old shower curtain that he had repurposed as reupholstering for his taxi's interior—a Middle Atlas version of a pimped-out ride. And so easy to clean!

I wished to keep the acrid diesel exhaust that invariably draped the highways of the country from entering the window. But only stubs remained where there should have been crank handles. I beckoned to Ahmed, who passed a handle to me. But soon after I acquired it, he attempted to point out something to me outside his window—a mountain formation or a pocket of ruins—but could not. I returned the handle so he could screw it back onto his door. That was when I discovered that his four-door taxi only had one crank handle. In lieu of a common language beyond simple French phrases, we developed a mutually intelligible crank gesture and spent the rest of the ride passing the handle back to each other. By the end of the drive, our pidgin sign language flowed with little thought required, and seemed as natural as any other.

—◦◦◦—

While peeking into the cafés of Meknès, I noticed a reality often repeated throughout Morocco: almost no women. In 1968, American expatriate writer Paul Bowles attempted to explain the dichotomy: "In a land whose social life is predicated on the separation of the sexes," he wrote without a hint of criticism, "the home is indisputably the woman's precinct; so the man must seek his life outside."

The patrons of the bar at the Hotel Rif, at the edge of Meknès' newer, French-designed quarter, looked elsewhere for inspiration. As a four-piece band was sweetly bounding through a jazzy shuffle, a jeans-clad medley of Moroccan women, sporting a noticeable but not excessive amount of makeup, stood, posed, and chatted—even though several couches were still free—waiting to dance when the urge would hit. Arabic and French chatter circulated around sips of Speciale Flag beer and mixed drinks. Everyone knew everyone else. Under the cover of a tourist bar, one with apparently no tourists other than me, Meknès' gathering of college-educated twenty-somethings swirled with unlocked energy. And about half the bargoers were women.

The band migrated to a style they fell into much more comfortably—Moroccan. Instantly, the horn-like keyboard voices swirled together with the solid groove of hand drums as a generous dose of reverb filled the room. Other guests kept tossing grins my way, as if to check up on me to make sure this newcomer was enjoying himself.

One of those was a woman at the bar feeding peanuts to her friends, and she began feeding them to me. Fatima, who spoke Arabic, Berber, French, and some Italian, described herself as part Berber and part Arabic. As the light caught the red highlights of her hair, her deep brown eyes remained on me when I spoke. Noticing that I had taken an interest in the band, Fatima began assisting me with identifying different styles of music that they had been playing. "This is Egyptian," she announced when the group's *doumbek* player trundled into an intense rhythm. The percussive sequence acted as a summons; a woman in a long skirt with an almost equally long slit rose up from one of the many couches and began belly dancing for a table of her friends.

A friend of Fatima's bobbed his way over to her, greeting her wide-mouthed in French. After a few words with her, he turned to me, steadying himself, and said what I am somewhat certain translated to "Beer with hashish will send you to the mountains!" I noted that both elements were in ample supply.

The band's next selection followed a more mechanical beat, accompanied by what sounded like a gritty rapping vocal in Arabic. "This is rai," Fatima declared carefully, as she fed me another peanut. The belly dancer grabbed a microphone and began trading verses with the band's male singer. With each hip twist, she gently radiated the song's waves of rhythm in the flattering amber light of the bar.

The smiles and handshakes toward me crescendoed as the patrons recognized that the chants of the rai music were captivating me. During the previous year, one of my last performances had been at the helm of a drum set at CBGB, in my hometown of New York City, its stage overlooking the standing room-only pit. The rai circulating through this bar tapped the same sense of belonging within me, albeit through a previously unknown back door.

I felt as if I were being adopted for the evening. Perhaps it was this unexpected conviviality, combined with the stream of beers and the hearty thump of the *doumbek*, that seized me from my barstool and sent me over to the band who was locked in a hypnotically steady instrumental break. The next moments melted into a single landscape of sensation—a gesture towards an unused hand drum, a new rhythm pattern my hands had found, a palpable current jumping from the hips of the dancers to the tips of my fingers.

After we ended the song on a tight slap of a note, the *doumbek* player embraced me in a sweaty, grinning hug, one I can still feel around me. In this sea of unfamiliarity, music found a way to open a channel of communication, a Moroccan evening of pleasure via the exchange of movement in place of syllables.

As I left, Fatima, a self-proclaimed Meknès resident, asked if I could give her 200 *dirhams*—the equivalent of about $20—for a cab ride home. I knew that copious sum could transport someone from Meknès to Tangier and back by train—an eight-hour round trip—and still leave some leftover change for a few croissants and a bottle of Poms soda. She reacted to my gentle refusal with pleading, burrowing eyes, but fell comfortably short of a need to kick me.

———

A week after I left Morocco, I called the hotel to find out what had become of the sweep. The police had found and arrested Alami, but since I was not in Fez to identify him at the time and no witnesses were able to do the same, they released him without charging him three days later.

Sometimes I wonder what I would have done if I were in Alami's moccasin-like leather shoes. I would love to claim that I'd have chosen to find a *doumbek* and some accomplices, place a donation jar on the ground and treat the street to song. But who knows—if I were born into such a trying society of 30 and 50 percent unemployment, maybe I would be slide-tackling tourists with a form worthy of a red card.

When I look at the tapestry that spun before me in Morocco up close, I see threads both maddening and enthralling. Haunting and just plain amusing. Alami is in there, of course, wrapped up with all the complexities and contradictions thriving in a land where one can speak French, English, Arabic, and Berber, but is hopelessly unemployed.

Following the threads then leads me to the memory of a music vendor in the Meknès Medina who rushed back to his kiosk to sell me the cassette of the energetic Orchestre Tahour he had been playing; or the man on the Fez-bound train who could not wait to discuss politics with me after I told him I was American ("Morocco has similar problems as America, very few people have the power," went his philosophy in baritone); or the student in Tangier whose face sparkled with delight when I'd given him a copy of my band's CD after he had helped me find my way through the city's repetition of cafés and concrete.

Attempting to step back and view the entire tapestry from a distance in hopes of discovering one all-encompassing design is daunting. If I zoom out, I lose the texture and detail of each moment, and in those details live the depths and dimensions of Morocco. With such textures lost, I might just jump to the most disturbing thread, and my most visceral thoughts would fill in the details. So I choose not to take in the whole but to dive into the rich, dense weave of threads.

In Search of *Baraka*

MJ Pramik

The distance runner is mysteriously reconciling the separations of body and mind, of pain and pleasure, of the conscious and the unconscious.

—George Sheehan in *Running &*
Being: The Total Experience

IN THE SPIRITUAL HAVEN of Fez, Morocco, I seek my father's *baraka*.

Baraka, the Sufis' breath of life or spiritual presence, is portrayed by ancient Islamic storytellers as a saintly old man in flowing robes, thin and gaunt under his twirled turban. The *baraka* unfolds the mystery of death to pilgrims on their way toward understanding.

As I walk through the courtyard of my *riad*, the white sunlight cascading into the center reminds me of the spark of light I witnessed at my father's last breath.

Far from my quaint Ohio birthplace, the Fez Medina embraces me with its mesmerizing shops, clanging metalware huts, spices that tease every sense at once, and the riot of color floating from scarves and cool geometric tiles. This World Heritage medina wanders and weaves. Black-dark, tight passages fill with donkeys, geese, chickens, grizzled-faced men shadowed in hoods of *djellabas*, and women veiled in *hijabs*.

Old men sit in doorways staring into the space before them. With unshaven jaws and furrowed foreheads, several faces stop me. They resemble my father in his ninth decade, solidly built with a ruddy complexion, crooked smile, and penetrating brown eyes.

I climb steep stairways of uneven stones. When I descend into shadowy, cavernous corridors, I feel as if I am on a journey into Hades. I recall the moment upon returning from a trip to Antarctica when I read the email from my youngest brother Michael urging me to hurry home to Ohio. Our father was fading fast.

Unknown to me, my siblings had decided to hasten my father's death by removing the intravenous fluid line. My sister and another brother both left town leaving Michael and me to care for our father.

"Why didn't you wait for me to remove the IV?" I asked, wounded. My father, a devout Catholic, had specified "resuscitate" in his will.

We moved Dad home and made him as comfortable as possible. Over five long days, I clutched his hand as his sturdy heart and strong lungs acquiesced to failing kidneys. His cadre of in-home caregivers sat vigil with us. My father smiled as we murmured stories of his ornery misdeeds. His feet turned black as his veins closed.

"Daddy, you had no business riding that lawnmower at ninety-one. You could have killed someone." He squeezed my fingers tight, his crooked smile feeble yet knowing.

His breathing grew ragged, abrupt, quick. At his last breath, a blinding cloud of iridescent light flew up and out of the window above his bed. It was nanosecond quick.

There's no instant replay in life. Time does not march on, it fleets, zaps, exhales . . . it's gone.

I did not say a proper goodbye to my "conscious" father, and I grieve this absence of leave-taking. But every place to which I travel, every distance to which I run, I sense my father's spirit, his breath of life.

I've met his soul in a Sri Lankan guide: Catholic and swarthy, dark-skinned like my father; I trusted him instantly. When, in St. Ives, Cornwall, a taxi driver, graying at the temples, said, "Call me, I'll come fetch you," I felt my father's *awen*, the Cornish/Druid term for spirit, the energy flow that is the essence of life. I felt the *rhohani*, or spirituality, of a Malaysian man, a dedicated Muslim who had twice carried out the *hajj* to Mecca. Something about the faraway look in his eye as he spoke to me made me trust his goodness as I had my father's.

And now, back at my *riad* in Fez, I sit alone in the courtyard. I recline upon pillows and gaze up four floors. The open space above me fills with a lightness of being. Blinded by the sunlight tumbling down, I feel a peace. This rendezvous with the spirit of my father in the gaunt faces of the medina's old men has calmed my ache to say goodbye.

His *baraka* lives here in these ancient walls. He holds me close and protects me.

My Criminal Career

Christina Ammon

IT WAS NEVER MY INTENTION to get involved in Morocco's underground drug trade. I lack a criminal disposition, and tangling with law enforcement and winding up in a foreign jail is not my idea of a thrill. It was the legal enchantments that drew me to Chefchouen: the mountains, the rivers, the blossoming almond trees.

But intention means very little in the labyrinthine medinas of Morocco. Set your GPS how you like, but you will soon find there are no routes, just blind corners; that you don't control your destiny so much as get dog-tired and wind up in situations: cornered by a guilt-wielding carpet seller, or trying on dozens of *djellabas* that you never even wanted and will for sure never wear.

My criminal career began and ended over a plate of gnocchi at The Mantra restaurant. The Mantra is one of those expat sanctuaries—there's one in every city—full of candles, bead curtains, low cushions, psychedelic art and lots of Bob Marley. I feel a little bad about these places because they are too easy and too wrongly removed from the local culture but, as I said before, the medina has a mind of its own and it delivers you where it will.

Besides, the familiarity of it was comforting. It was the off-season and a difficult time to be a solo traveler. The weather was cold and the main square near empty. I'd spent the whole morning admiring traveling couples who perched together on the walls around the old Mosque, and drinking mint tea at café tables. They had the posture of contented people: self-contained and satiated. I, on the other hand, hadn't spoken to anyone in a week. My boyfriend, Andy, would catch up soon and although the alone time had been beneficial—I always become a poet in the quiet drift of solitude—the need for human contact drove me out this one day, eyes wide open, looking for an in.

I followed the host of The Mantra restaurant to the top floor, and when I crested the staircase, I was happy to hear English spoken. Three men, each seated at a separate table, all looked up to greet me—in English—before getting back to their business: one scrolled an iPod, another worked a sketch, and a third leaned back on a low corner couch.

The room had a vague haze. Smoke. I looked for a source. Burnt chicken *tagine*? Incense? Did we need to call for a fire extinguisher?

"Welcome," exhaled a man in purple pants. A plume of smoke swirled around his beard. "Martin. From Scotland."

Chefchouen is famous for the marijuana—or *kif*—that thrives in surrounding mountains. Though technically illegal, it's proffered and smoked openly and a mainstay of the rural economy. It took me a while to see it out in plain sight, partly because I wasn't looking for it.

What I *was* looking for was a glass of wine—which in Morocco holds the opposite status than pot: though technically legal, Mohammed forbids drinking in the Koran, and his law—in the minds of many—is mightier than any secular law. On Internet forums, travelers sought advice on where to score a bottle in Chefchouen, but the discussion threads led nowhere. Meanwhile, there were huge rounds of fresh goat cheese for sale in the street markets just begging for a glass of *vino tinto*.

I sat down at a corner table. The menu was an eclectic tome of Italian, Chinese and Moroccan. I turned in my chair.

"What's good to eat here?"

"Everything" Martin said, exhaling another plume of smoke. Then he clarified: to be honest, it was hearsay. He couldn't afford any of it. After five years living in Chefchouen, he'd achieved a nearly cash-free existence, living on a nearby farm and growing veggies for bartering. He just waited at The Mantra on market day to catch a ride back to the farm.

I ordered blue cheese gnocchi and looked around the room. We chatted. The man scrolling the iPod was a DJ from Ireland. Recently divorced, he'd spent the last two weeks snuggling with a water bottle, smoking *kif*, and snacking his way through the medina munchies. The other guy was Jonah. He was the owner. He rarely looked up from his Bic pen drawing, except to take an intermittent puff from his chillum and to show us the picture he was working on: a couple of elaborately intertwined snakes.

I'd been told that owning a restaurant was at least as stressful as being a heart surgeon, but Jonah made it look easy—doodling, smoking, and changing the stereo tracks from Ray Charles to John Lee Hooker. His Moroccan waiter, meanwhile, ran the show. Martin would later tell me that Jonah was navigating a heartbreak with *kif* and his drawings which papered the walls, hung midair from thread mobiles, and covered the menus.

My gnocchi arrived—blue cheese and almonds in a clay *tagine* dish. I dug in and it was excellent, but would have been so much more so with a glass of Merlot. "You want a hit off this?" Martin extended his pipe. I held up my hand: No thanks. The smoke-choked air alone made me high.

"What I really want is a glass of wine."

"Good luck. You won't find it here. This town is bone dry."

Martin invited me to his farm and I went the next day. He and the owner, Rachid, prepared a fish *tagine* in slow epochs, the cutting and passing of each ingredient into the clay pot the passage of a geologic age. Between episodes, they smoked *kif*, laughed a lot, and got distracted by other chores: picking up rocks, gathering wood. I followed Rachid around and we toured the farm: the onions, the garlic, the oncoming snap peas. Eventually we ate and I was grateful. In return, I invited Martin to dinner at The Mantra the following night.

Before meeting Martin at the restaurant, I'd planned a three-hour hike with a guide named Achmed who I'd met in the square. Achmed and I followed a wide road up the mountain above town, stopping at a the top for a view and a cup of mint tea. Then, instead of going down the nice clean trail in front of us, Achmed suggested we go over the lip of the mountain.

I balked. "What about the time?" I asked, reminding him of my 7:00 meet-up at The Mantra with Martin.

He promised: "No problem No problem."

Two hours later the sun was setting as we picked our way, heads down, through the slippery scree on the other side of the mountain. My ankles were twisted and my knees were hammered. When we at last reached the road, men in *djellabas* passed us with donkeys on the return route to their mountain villages. The sky turned grenache-pink and Venus blinked on but I was too peeved to appreciate it. The hike was supposed to be three hours and we were pushing five.

I walked with a slight limp and when we rounded a bend, the lights of town seemed impossibly far.

"Another hour to town," Achmed said. I tripped in a pothole and began to sniffle. I wanted to sit down on that road and never get up.

"Ah Christina . . ." he consoled. "Christina I am sorry. Take my hand . . ."

And in what I can only explain now as some sort of Stockholm syndrome setting in, I actually reciprocated, grasping Achmed's hand and allowing him to lead me down the mountain, strangely consoled and annoyed at the same time.

The band of light on the horizon had now darkened to the color of a deep cabernet. I thought of my dinner and then remembered: another wine-less Italian meal. "Achmed, I wish I could find wine in this town!"

He was eager to help. "This I can find for you." My spirits brightened and my limp vanished.

When we arrived in town, we skirted the medina for another mile. At last he stopped at an unmarked door. "You go." He stood back and motioned me forward. I pushed open the heavy wooden door.

Inside the smoky din men bellied up to the bar and drank frothy beers. There was music and good cheer. A tall European stood behind the bar, a red light illuminating his bald head.

"A bottle," I ventured.

"Red or White?"

"Red."

He slid it into a plastic bag and we slid that bag into my canvas bag and I paid him. It was that easy.

I would arrive at The Mantra late, but Martin was already up in smoke. Jonah was sitting in the same chair transfixed by his chillum and a new Bic pen masterpiece. He ok-ed the wine, so long as we drank it on the low table behind the partition and kept it discreet out of respect for his staff. He rustled me up an opener.

I lowered onto the couch, knees throbbing and face wind-chapped and sun-reddened. I held the contraband under the table and pulled the cork.

Martin was impressed. "I've lived in Chefchouen five years and had no idea . . ."

I ordered the gnocchi again and we toasted under the table. While he freely exhaled lung-fulls of *kif*, I nursed my wine in discreet sips which forbidden tasted better.

Martin's conversation was as meandering as the medina, drifting from subject to subject like an aimless cloud and waylaying me in an eventual white-out. I was too tired to care whether he made sense or not. Mostly I just leaned back and felt proud of myself; I'd infiltrated the underground wine trade of Chefchouen in five days flat and rather liked the sensation of being a criminal. "If you are not a 'minor' criminal of some sort in this day and age one is not truly living," my friend Pat has said.

In the ensuing days, I would acquire this x-ray vision, an ability to see beyond the surfaces of things—to the underworld ways that animal appetites find outlet: to threadbare cats hunched over dark-street dumpsters, to young couples kissing among tombstones at the cemetery on the edge of town. I learned which boulder shielded the heroin junkies and spied a fist-fight breaking in the alley just as the five-o'clock prayers sounded from the mosque.

Andy would arrive soon, and I'd have my nose out of trouble. Mischief courts only the solo traveler. I'd miss my criminal days, but be happy for the sobriety and the coherent conversation and a different sort of mischief. Until then, I had a half a bottle of wine left, a round of goat cheese, and the sweet free sensation of having let my law-abiding, politically-correct self take a wrong turn in the medina of Chefchouen, all for a glass of Cabernet.

Tradition

That, when you come down to it is the only kind of courage that is demanded of us: the courage for the oddest, the most unexpected, the most inexplicable things that we may encounter.

—Rainer Maria Rilke, *Letters to a Young Poet*

My *Habibi*
MJ Pramik

After the Diwan of Alim Maghrebi

Habibi
you are the shaking, gnarled hand seizing my breath
you ask I surrender to the blackness from which you emerge

Habibi
you are the left hand that steadies the coarse medina wall
your grey *djellaba* sleeve folds down to reveal still taught
sinews

Habibi
you are the one I've been waiting for, your vacant eyes
capture me with flares of light setting this dark passage ablaze

Habibi
you are the palm, the oasis, the pink dunes at sunset
I have not seen, nor will see, on this journey to your land

and you remain always the outstretched right hand curving to cradle
the orange with its leaves still attached that I so gently
lay against your tanned calloused skin

Extract from *A Very Private Jihad*

Sandy McCutcheon

The extract tells the story of a trip into the deepest part of the medina of Fez where the narrator has his senses taken over by the female djinn (djinniya), *Aisha Kandisha*

FINALLY I FELT STRONG enough to venture out and I will never forget that day. It was as if I was seeing the medina for the first time. To others I must have appeared a madman. My beard and hair were long and untamed, my beloved black *djellaba* more than a little frayed, yet I couldn't have cared less.

Walking with the stumbling, shuffling gait of the well practiced insomniac—a dreamer half woken, the woken half sleeping—I traced a path through the streets to the Sagha *funduq*. Here I was forced to stop, my senses assaulted by familiar wild magic. There was no time for me to resist, even if such resistance had been possible. *She* was showing me her power. *She* was saying, *look what I can do, even in broad daylight.*

History swirled around me, dizzying, disorienting until the kaleidoscope slowed and the *caravanserai* doors swung open, allowing its ghosts to roam the present. The sounds of the past revived; the coughing of long dead camels, the braying of a donkey protesting the weight of sheepskins, a rooster calling from high on a terrace wall and the shouted greetings of travellers reunited after the long journeys from Marrakech, Timbuktu or beyond. Goods came and went on camel or donkey train, on mules, or carried by black slaves; men from Africa, huge beasts of burden, whose scarred bodies bent beneath the weight of merchandise or the live animals slung around their necks.

Rough, cloth-wrapped bundles, wooden packing cases, rolled carpets; all were being unpacked, repacked, inspected, bought, sold or haggled over. In front of giant scales, big enough to weigh a man, a queue was formed, sellers and buyers anxious to check the weights and close the deals.

Three Jews from Lihoudi sat huddled in discussion, ignoring the sea of hands offering baubles, beads, cakes, pastries, herbs or *kif*, for their minds were on more precious cargo; spices from India, fine silks from Persia, Syrian silver, Iraqi glass. Their skin and even their eyes were the colour of gold, for these men were goldsmiths, whose days and nights were filled with the glow and dust of their trade. Their sweat was an amalgam and even as they slept the metal seeped through their pores, which is why, it was said, they never went to the hammam or gave their washing out, but kept it at home where their wives could retrieve the valuable deposit of their perspiration and their dreams.

Glasses of tea, of coffee, of camel's milk were trotted back and forth by boys, their simple *djellabas* stained with the badges of their trade. The noise was intense, a babble of languages, of accents, dialects, of grunts and groans, of coughing, spitting and curses.

Laughter too, a woman's, issuing from behind a window grill, high up, the notes wafting like feathers into the square below.

A cry went up and people turned to stare as a wealthy merchant came from l'Marqtane in Achebine, with three newly purchased slaves roped together. All were young attractive women, two with the blue-black skin of the Nubians, the third as pale as longing, her red hair tossed over her shoulder, the remnants of her Irish skirt protruding beneath the hem of a cheap shift thrown on for decency. Unbowed like her African sisters, she held her head high and met my gaze; insouciance her only defence.

That these were ghosts mattered little, for the door between the worlds was now wide open and I allowed myself to flow with the history until it took me up some stairs to the present, to a tea shop where I sat with old men on dusty carpets and drank mint tea and shared a pipe.

See what you will lose if you abandon me.

Her voice in my head was accompanied by a quivering ache that had me holding my head in my hands.

'I will never abandon you,' I said out loud.

The old man beside me on the rug, lifted his pipe in salute. *'Ma'fehmt,'* he cackled, his liquid laugh emerging from between toothless gums.

'I don't understand either,' I replied. And it was true. Why would I abandon her, even if such a thing were possible?

Two Muhammads

Lisa Alpine

"I WANT SON JUST LIKE THIS!" *Thump, thump, thump.*

Galen's chest resounded like a Taiko drum as the turbaned, mustachioed man in a long, pale-blue robe pounded my son's back with his palm. The Berber tribal leader raised him high, showing the other men in the lantern-lit tent our eight-month-old baby. *"Willy Muhammad! Willy Muhammad!"* he yelled as he pumped Galen up and down. Stubby legs dangling and tiny hands flapping, Galen chortled.

Usually reluctant to let strangers hold him—especially loud and hairy folk—for some reason the tall chieftain didn't scare Galen. His blue eyes gazed steadily at the throng of men admiring his magnificent, infant-sized rib cage and chest.

They escorted Andy, my husband, and me out and closed the flaps. Chanting emanated from within the massive slate-black tent. I stood on alert, waiting to spring forward if I heard a cry or a whimper. When I peeked in, he was sitting on a Berber rug in the center of a ring of dark-eyed men, who drummed on taut goatskin *tars*. As the adoring circle of clansmen swayed in a rhythmic trance around him, Galen watched them with utter equanimity, enjoying his princely role.

How did our blond baby end up being serenaded in a Berber tent high in the Atlas Mountains?

My husband and I were travel writers, and we often ported Galen nonchalantly to remote corners of the globe. This time, we'd packed his toys, diapers, and strollers, and trundled him onto the Royal Air Maroc flight from New York to Marrakech.

A fellow traveler had piqued our interest with the story of an ancient tribal festival in Morocco in a region in the middle of nowhere with no hotels or paved roads. We decided this would be the perfect destination for our next off-the-beaten-path-adventure-with-a-baby.

The Imilchil Betrothal Fair has been held annually for millennia in the heart of the High Atlas Mountains. Every September, neighboring tribes gather in a festival in which women are allowed to "choose" their husbands. The legend is that two young lovers, forbidden to see each other by their warring families, cried themselves to death, and their tears formed the lakes of Isli ("his") and Tislit ("hers") near Imilchil. Chastened, the families dedicated a day every year on the anniversary of the lovers' deaths on which people of different tribes could marry each other of their own free will.

Thousands of Berber tribesmen travel to Imilchil by camel, horse, donkey, and jeep to socialize and pair up their children—a tribal "Dating Game" with dowries. Woven camel hair tents are set up, the Berbers smoke hookahs, cook, trade, and fire antique muskets into the sky—their celebratory equivalent of fireworks—while lamb *tagines* simmer over fires.

After landing in Marrakech, we drove north to Fez—the gateway city to the mountains where the festival is held.

After settling into a hotel, with Galen and his road-weary father asleep, I wandered down to the bar, where a dashing man in a khaki safari outfit came over and introduced himself.

"*Bonsoir*, my name is Driss."

Driss was a geologist who had been educated in England and currently lived in Paris. He had been born in a cave deep in the Atlas while his father's tribe fought the French to gain independence in the 1950s. He told me of growing up with real rifles and daggers for toys.

I asked what he was doing in Fez. "I'm going to visit my father up in the Atlas," he said. "We're going to the Imilchil Betrothal Fair."

I told him I was going there as well. Driss doubted the rental car would make it. "It is very dangerous. The *wadis* have flash floods, the streambeds are already full."

He offered to take me. I didn't add that I was with my family, with enough baby accoutrements to open a Toys R Us.

The next morning, I bundled up our rosy-cheeked, sleep-kissed son and nursed him while Andy packed our gear.

When Driss joined us in the lobby, he looked astonished to see an infant and a husband and a mountain of overstuffed duffel bags.

We crammed ourselves into his highly polished Land Rover and started driving toward the mountain range looming to the east. As I discreetly stuck Galen's head under my blouse, I caught sight, in the rear-view mirror, of Driss' Groucho Marx eyebrows knitted in horror.

But I could tell he was delighted and amused by our whimsical trip to the Atlas with a baby.

Driss pointed out caverns where his father had hidden while fighting the French. We begged him for details of his warring, nomadic youth. He guided us along the stony trails where he had herded livestock up to high-altitude mountain pastures, where he discovered the veins of crystals and fossils that had inspired him to become a geologist.

The road was ripped by water troughs, slippery with scree. Large boulders were expertly skirted. We climbed a stair-case-like route—narrow, muddy, rutted. The jeep jolted and jounced through ravines of striated pink and yellow rock.

As Galen dozed, lulled by the rocking ride, Driss asked, "Why do you travel with your baby and all this luggage to places far away from your home?"

"We're nomads at heart and are happiest when wandering in foreign cultures," I said. "Luckily, our son seems to enjoy it, too."

Driss smiled. "We are very much alike. I love foreign cultures. I hope I will meet a wife who wants to travel with our children—but it will probably not be at Imilchil—so don't get any ideas!"

At dusk, we reached the lip of the rift, known as the "Plateau des Lacs," at an elevation of 2,119 meters. A scene from *One Thousand and One Nights* throbbed below in the mile-long valley of Assif Melloul ("white river"). Thousand-head herds of horses, camels, and goats milled about, restlessly stomping, their pawing hoofs raising a taupe-tinted veil of dust. Bleating and hawing drifted upward in a cacophony of sounds highlighted by hoots, rifle fire, cymbals, and banging drums. A legion of black tents cut a swath through the center of a valley pulsing with revelry.

Galen seemed to sense this phantasmagorical scene pulling us downward onto the alluvial plain. I held him up and he screeched in delight at the mayhem. When we reached the outskirts of the encampment, he bounced up and down holding onto the window edge, excited to see the cartoonish bearded camels flirtatiously blinking their long lashes. Swaggering Berbers sporting curved daggers gathered around our vehicle, peering in at the foreigners. We slowly drove into the vortex and stopped.

Doors flew open, and Driss was pulled out of the jeep by brothers and cousins and uncles. He introduced us to the relatives that poured forth to slap his back and raise eyebrows in our direction. Galen was swept up by the tribal leader, who was eager to introduce him to his comrades in the grand meeting tent.

Driss didn't seem fazed that Galen was being carried off with exuberant fanfare, so we weren't either. While he set up camp, he encouraged us to follow Galen's entourage.

As Andy and I waited outside the tent, the temperature plummeted and high winds delivered face-slapping, bone-chilling blasts. A silver moon rose from behind the ragged mountain peaks.

Driss insisted that Galen and I sleep in the inner tent sanctum on his bedroll with most of the blankets and sheep-skins he had brought for himself. He and Andy headed for the outer tent, wearing all their clothes to keep warm. They stayed up, pacing around the bonfires, drinking scalding mint tea while volleys of rifle fire crackled through the hoarfrost, encrusting the starry night air. Sleep eluded all except Galen, who sank into baby oblivion.

The next morning, with Galen perched in a pack on Andy's back, we wandered through the maze of tents, everything covered in a fine silt that had been stirred up by the horses that galloped through camp, their riders whooping and hollering while waving muskets above their heads.

Warrior blood flows through the Berbers' veins. Berber is derived from the Latin word "Barbari," or barbarians—a title given to them almost 2,000 years ago by invading Roman armies, who were repeatedly attacked by a race of fiercely independent tribes. Many Berbers call themselves some variant of the word *imazighen,* meaning "free people" or "free and noble men," and their symbol is that of a man holding his arms to the sky—a free man. A man who will not be conquered.

Later, we were ushered into another tent by a group of tittering women bedecked in silver jewelry, their eyes rimmed in kohl, with geometric, smoky-blue tattoos on their face, hands, and feet. Driss had told us that some Berber tribes tattoo a woman's chin to indicate whether she is married or divorced, and if she has any children. Some tribes believe that the tattooed symbols provide protection from evil. He also shared that French colonial scholars, in their search for the origins of Berber art, suggested that North African Berber tattoos resembled Neolithic pictograms in caves in Spain.

Up until now, the Berbers had seemed delighted to have us in their midst but suddenly, a woman was yammering at me and wagging her finger in Andy's direction. The other women in the tent concurred. We were obviously doing something wrong, but what? Driss was off helping his father trade horses and bargain for rifles, so we didn't have our translator to clarify why we were causing such a stir.

My gaze followed the direction of the women's pointing fingers and narrowed eyes, landing on Galen, who was in the pack on Andy's back. The women continued to *tsk*, poke and pull on my sleeve, pointing at Andy and Galen.

Ahhh—the man should not be carrying the baby. That was my job.

I transferred Galen to my back, then the women gestured for us to sit on the rug for tea. It was an elaborate process that involved pouring scalding water in a high stream into the teapot over seven different kinds of herbs—wild mint, thyme, lemongrass, geranium, sage, verbena, and a hint of absinthe wormwood—and three or four generous clumps of raw sugar. After serving us, the women went back to their chores, humming and murmuring softly.

It was busy under the eaves of this open-sided tent. As I jiggled Galen on my lap, men sharpened daggers and scythes on whetstones; women in ornately embroidered black dresses trudged in, carrying amphorae of sloshing water on their backs; babies crawled over every faded orange, red, and green wool rug overlapped on the floor; and the older children stared in wonder at Galen's corn silk hair.

The next day we were invited to share a meal with Driss's extended clan. Aromas of greasy grilling lamb and savory *tagines* mingled with the sharp odor of camel dung, smoke, and dust that hung like a thick cloud throughout the tent.

One of Driss's distant cousins had a gorgeous baby about Galen's size. She had huge doe eyes framed in kohl, eyelashes thick and black, mocha skin, and a wind-chime laugh. Engraved and beaded bracelets adorned her pudgy arms.

I admired her beauty and the mother held her out for me to hold as I passed Galen to her.

Galen and the little girl clasped hands and were juxtaposed light and dark mirror images.

The tribe gathered around, cooing over the two babies. We laughed and agreed how adorable they were together. They batted their eyelashes, flirting.

The parents made playful, suggestive gestures about the two becoming engaged, and Driss said teasingly, "They think we should marry them here at Imilchil today when the governor flies in to officiate the group marriage ceremony. Everyone is exclaiming they are a perfect match."

Andy and I laughed. We had to agree—our babies were a good-looking couple. Meanwhile, Galen was leaning toward his new girlfriend, trying to plant a gooey kiss and embrace her in a wobbly hug. She beamed and seemed amenable to this new-found baby love.

Curious, I said, "Driss, ask them what their child's name is."

The father proudly intoned, "Muhammad."

The parents then pointed to Galen, inquiring what "her" name was.

I froze, the sea of expectant, smiling faces making my face flush. "Um . . . his name . . . is . . . Muhammad . . . ?"

The temperature in the tent grew frosty as the baby's mother and father grabbed little Muhammad from my arms and stalked off, deeply offended that we had mistaken their firstborn son for a lowly girl.

Driss pulled us out of the tent in a hurry without saying goodbye to his cousins, who glowered.

Once out of earshot, he said, "Well, that was embarrassing! Guess I will stay out of the marriage broker business."

We wandered to the epicenter of the festivities, where a large stage had been set up. Several dozen teenage couples in full ceremonial regalia shyly wandered through the crowd, holding hands. The young girls in a flurry of fabrics, headdresses, and jewelry; the young men—many shorter than their brides-to-be—in white shirts and pants, daggers dangling from their belts.

Galen slept soundly in the pack on my back, a blanket draped over his head to protect him from the high winds and also to ensure that he would not be mistaken for a marriageable girl-child.

Tribal flags snapped in the gusts. A helicopter buzzed across the valley and landed near the stage in a frenzy of clapping and the ubiquitous rifle fire.

The copter's rotary blades kicked up tornados of bone-dry silt, which hovered about the debarking governor like a mystical shroud. With great fanfare he brushed the dust off his satin baseball jacket and mounted the stage, holding a bullhorn. Over all the chaotic noise, he gave a speech, then announced that the couples were now man and wife. Everyone dispersed, and Driss herded us back to the jeep, as he was in a hurry to catch his flight home to Paris that evening.

Back at the hotel in Fez, Driss helped us load our mammoth pile of baby items into the rental car. Saying goodbye, he reached out to hold Galen, gave him a squeeze, and bounced him up and down. Galen grasped Driss's thumb and sucked on it. Gazing into my son's lake-blue eyes, Driss solemnly said, "Little Muhammad, I really enjoyed meeting you. I hope my son will be brave and strong, but not as pretty as you."

A Berber musician friend of mine recently looked mystified when I asked him what "Willy Muhammad" meant, describing the scene when Galen was prince of the tent show. I yelled it just like I remember the mustachioed chieftain doing as he hefted Galen above his head for the turbaned Berbers to admire. Puzzled, Khaled scratched his balding head and then said, "No, no. not 'Willy,' silly! They must have been saying 'Wahedlee Muhammad,' which means, *'Oh, little Muhammad!"*

Postcards

And it did have a terrace with one of the most spectacular views in Fez, all the way down the valley to the Atlas Mountains. The panorama was breathtaking: hills covered with cube-shaped houses to the left, sweeping down to Mount Zalagh. Here and there were the spires of minarets. In the far distance was a plume of black smoke from the potteries, which burned olive pits as fuel in the kilns. If you removed the satellite dishes, the view could have been straight out of the Old Testament.

—Suzanna Clarke, *A House in Fez*

Ablution Room

Claire Fallou

THE LIGHT IS SOFT AND LOW in the men's underground ablution room below the Hassan II Mosque in Casablanca. It falls in golden shafts through holes in the ceiling, blurred by a veil of steam that leaves the remote corners in half-darkness. The white and green mosaics glisten softly on the walls and floor, waiting.

"Men must come here to wash before prayer," the guide explains. "That ritual is called *wudu*."

Overgrown marble mushrooms as high as my hip are sprouting from the ground, dozens of them, evenly spaced apart in the wide green area. The place feels like a dark, damp forest, with slender beige columns holding a low vaulted ceiling. The citrus fragrance of argan soap lingers over vestiges of acrid male sweat. Hollows in the hand-crafted clay tiles are shiny with water that shivers to the muffled beat of our slow steps.

Gliding through the dampness, I follow their gentle ripples to the silent end of the room.

Men come here every morning, drawn by the *muezzin's* guttural chant vibrating across the city's transparent sky. The same dark-skinned men whose defiant gazes search for mine, then shy away, when we cross in the streets.

I know a man back home in Paris whose luminous sea-green eyes sometimes hold mine for long moments. I am the one who always shies away then.

In swift motions those men take off their shoes and shirts and kneel before the mushroom fountains. The water flows along the smooth marble curves onto their backs and shoulders, filling the creases and shining on the honey-colored expanses. They soap their hands thrice, their faces thrice, their feet thrice as Allah commands, rinsing from their minds the picture of their curvy women splashing next door in their own ablution room.

The men greet the inner peace that stems from a deep certainty of their own place in a greater order.

He is here now. One among them, ivory-skinned among the dark complexions. In measured moves he raises his cupped hands for water, presses them to his face.

He has felt my presence, as he always does. He lifts his face up to me.

Once again, his almond-shaped eyes catch my own. All I see now is a quiet green ocean dancing with specks of gold and longing shadows. My stomach tightens as he blinks like a caress through black eyelashes.

Leaning against a column I shut my lids and breathe out in the black.

The guide's voice drones on, somewhere far away. The column is strong against my back, holding me like a man would.

Like he would.

He stands up and steps towards me. Breathless I search his gaze again and hold it this time. Under his light, my defiance slowly melts away. My yearning swirls inside of me, light and free for the first time, bringing a smile to my lips. It fills me, floats out and crosses the ablution room to meet his own desire.

Yes.

The steam dissolves and I see.

Maison Arabesque

Amy Gigi Alexander

MAISON ARABESQUE. THE name sounded liquid and romantic, and I could not help but reserve rooms there months in advance just because of the name alone. I was planning a trip to Tangier, a city I had visited previously.

Tangier and I had a long history: I had come across several books in my youth written by Mohamed Choukri, who had grown up in the slums of the city and had taught himself to write. He eventually wrote about many of the glittering literati who frequented or lived in the city: Paul Bowles, Jean Genet, and Tennessee Williams. But it was not his stories about parties, prostitution, or port-thieves that drew me in: it was his thoughts on writing, for he said that words could be a tool: a way to expose, to protest and to save oneself. In my teenage years, to read this was like receiving manna, and I ate everything he wrote greedily, almost obsessively. We had many of the same burdens of childhood, and his liberation became mine, although I never acted on it in the same way. It was through his books that I discovered Tangier, which seemed at once a dark place full of shadowed dealings, but also strangely attractive, a whirling dervish of creativity.

In my thirties, I finally had my chance to go to Tangier, for I was in Spain and it was a simple ferry ride across the divide. Wishing to be solitary, I choose a seat that was isolated far from the group of tourists that boarded at the same time. From the moment I sat down the men gathered around me, talking and making jokes, and then leaning in close. I decided if I could hold out until I reached the harbor, I would be all right. There I would find the city of Choukri: crushed cobalt underfoot, stained fingertips, midnight conversation, hidden places—but mixed with the heavy scent of gardenia and lemon leaves, a haiku to the creative freedom I so desperately wanted.

I left the dock and boarded a taxi for the center of the city, and when we arrived at the Grand Socco square, I got out and wandered, looking for vestiges of Choukri. The famous square was not a square at all, but an arc, tightly surrounded by shops and crumbling sandstone sidewalks filled with people. In the center was a fountain, and surrounding it were benches and grassy plantings on which lovers and tourists were examining maps, smoking hashish, or making out in equal measure.

It was a layered chaos that was loud, frustrated, peeled, dangerous. Midnight-colored things. Children blistered, glassy. Men with tracked arms argued in the street. It was everything

Tennessee Williams described, "A true document of human desperation, shattering in its impact." I had both expected this darkness and wished for it not to be. I was not ready to lose my innocence, did not want to see this part of life. Hurt and stunned, I ran, without looking where I was going, back onto the boat which took me across the sea, having lasted only a single afternoon in the city that had promised so much. Not once did I turn around to say goodbye to Tangier.

Yet, Tangier left its handprint on my back. In between the black holes of people forgotten and forgetting, there were things there I had never seen anywhere else, images which filled my mind long after I left. Bougainvillea, with its violet prose, as it exploded vibrant up tiled walls. The gardenia blooms floating on water in aluminum tubs in the flower market. The white gateway to the sea, turquoise and dotted with candy-gem sailboats of red and pink, a salt infused breath away from the stench of confetti-like trash that covered the beach. Sweet and bitter mandarins, so small I had filled my bag with dozens of them and eaten each segment as I had walked around the city, stuffing their peelings in my pockets.

Years later, I was still dreaming of violet leaves airbrushed blue-pink-red blending under light so bright it woke me up. In a cigar box, hidden deep in my closet, was a browned bundle of gardenia petals which had not lost their smell and the remnants of mandarin peels which had not lost their color. Tangier could not be forgotten, and one day, it called me to return.

I found Maison Arabesque through a friend: I was shown a single photograph of a creamy-yellow rooftop with palms and plumed ferns in cobalt-blue pots, and in the background a city flat and stretching, every space filled. I could picture myself on that rooftop, eating mandarins and drinking tea dotted with orange blossoms.

I was also attracted by the story of the house and its owner, Peter, who on his first visit to Tangier had been struck madly with feverish love for the city, the invitation to lose oneself. Peter had accepted what the city had offered, and found Maison Arabesque. The house was originally built for a merchant in 1898, and had been handed over several times, each new owner covering it with another layer of paint, hiding the lady within. Peter bought her, and spent years discovering who she was, bringing her back to her original appearance.

I arrived with a suitcase and my pockets lined with the aged tangerine peels and gardenia petals of years ago: I sensed they would serve me as talismans of good luck and compass both. As I got off the plane, into the taxi, and finally arrived at the Grand Socco, where I would meet Peter, I held the petals and peels until they were damp, full of trepidation that I might run away once again.

Peter stood waiting on the edge of the square. He was tall and thin and lean: he looked like he both belonged and didn't belong to Tangier at the same time. Blonde and fair, he smiled widely, laughing in greeting. His laugh was Moroccan, warm and abundant, but his face was from Amsterdam. He grabbed my bags and walked quickly through a maze, away from the big open square of the city and into a collection of arched recessed alleyways which led to Maison Arabesque.

And then there she was. Her door was like any other door in that lane, and on one side was a shop of badly painted Moroccan crockery, the sort of shop busloads of tourists are taken to buy ashtrays and dishes that they will display but never use. The steps into the house were uneven, and the wooden carved doors with faded symbols heavy, with several large keyholes and what looked to be a lock from the Middle Ages. Peter opened the doors, and we went in.

Oh, she was perfect. Outside, it was tight and the tall buildings made the alley dim; but inside, it was supernaturally glowing, with a natural light that came down into the foyer like cascading curls of white waves. The froth of the sea, airborne, filtering through a single skylight, choosing her inner rooms as its sanctuary.

I had an immediate sense that the house was not merely a house, but a living, breathing organism which groaned and shifted and sighed. As we walked over black and white tiles, up a wrought iron staircase that twirled as though it was going up into the sky, Peter said, "The house chooses her guests."

My room was the Palm d'Or: the room of golden palms, a styled art deco Moroccan dream. Cream and wood. Sage and lavender brushed tiles. Photographs of men and women in rough robes and jewels. Black, white, sepia. The windows were covered with floor to ceiling shutters, and one window looked out on the house across the way, where I could see into a room and glimpse part of a stairwell. The Palm d'Or was in the front of the house, and these windows were her eyes into the street.

As soon as the door was closed, I sat down in a chair and waited. I almost felt I needed the permission of the house to walk around freely, to touch things. Then a shutter opened slightly, a push from the breeze or perhaps the house herself, and I went to the window. I was unseen, just as the house herself was unseen, watching as she always had done.

Below, four boys played marbles right in the center of the alley, and a fish-cart man, followed by a group of orange cats, waited patiently together for the game to end so they could continue. A rush of women walking, flowered headscarves, holding thin plastic bags of greens and bundles of pink carnations, their spice wafting into my room. The house on the opposite side of the street was so close I could almost touch it. There was a small window which showed an occasional blur of women's feet, as they walked quickly up and down the stairs, red and blue plastic flip-flops that hit the tiled stairs flapping. The sight of their bare heels seemed painfully intimate, and I looked away, to the lace curtains on the window, which moved as the women walked past.

I kept the shutters opened and turned off the lights, lay on the bed in my clothes, and listened to the night sounds of Tangier. Call to prayer, buzzed singsong. Metal against metal, unknown clash and clatter. A buzzer rang for someone to be let in. Doors slammed. Cheers, from a soccer game down the alleyway, rode in and out of the windows like a roar, each time there was a goal. And later, smaller sounds, intimate ones: someone dropped their keys; a drunken man stumbled and shuffled; a child wailed as a woman yelled; the paws of a dog click-clacked on the cobblestones; the waves of the sea rocked the house gently and it creaked with each ebb.

In the morning, I awoke, having dreamt of ships the whole night, and felt as though I was wrapped in sinew and tissues and curved bent wood. I was part of Maison Arabesque, which was in two places at the same time: planted solidly in Tangier, and aloft on the oceans.

Through a tiny entrance almost hidden, I wandered up, turning my feet sideways on narrow stairs, and walked out onto the creamy-yellow rooftop. Buttercup mixed with green and blooms. In the center were a series of windows that appeared to move, glass thrown against the wall and landing in perfect precision: poppy, azure, mustard and silver glinting splinted views of the city which surrounded us below.

The city below was afloat on blue, its buildings stacked high and rambling, clothes strung to dry on lines like masts and flags. On an adjoining rooftop, a gardenia shrub shone, leggy and dark green, with one single blossom. I took a deep breath as the scent filled my body, as I reached into my pocket for a mandarin. Its peel slid off easily and I ate it, as I leaned against the wall of Maison Arabesque.

Through my eyes, Tangier and I had both changed, with our beauty outshining our darkness this time.

Comme un Bébé

Marguerite Richards

Comme un bébé.
Like a baby, she said,
as she covered my head with a coarse towel
patting my hair dry
in the wet heat of the hammam.
Mais ça fait longtemps que tu n'es plus un bébé.
But it's been a while since you've been a baby, she
gently scolded.
I could take care of myself now.
Relinquishing my power to a man is not the same as
honoring him.
She continued to pat my face dry,
watching me intently with her deep brown eyes.
She had scrubbed my body hard,

scrubbed me clean of yesterday.

Tu vois?

You see? She asked.

She pointed to my dead skin,

now a hundred dark particles,

sloughed off,

the muck of my mistake,

washing down the drain.

Maintenant tu oublies.

Va t'allonger un peu.

Now you forget, she said.

Rest a bit.

Wisdom

From far off, through circuitous corridors, came the scent of citrus-blossom and jasmine, with sometimes a bird's song before dawn, sometimes a flute's wail at sunset, and always the call of the muezzin in the night . . .

To visit Morocco is still like turning the pages of some illuminated Persian manuscript all embroidered with bright shapes and subtle lines.

—Edith Wharton, *In Morocco*

Beneath the Almond Tree

Candace Rose Rardon

A single act of kindness throws out roots in all directions, and the roots spring up and make new trees.

—Amelia Earhart

ROSES AREN'T SUPPOSED to let you down.

Neither are rose festivals, one of which had drawn my friend Liz and me to Morocco's Valley of Roses one May. There wasn't much written online about the festival, but what the guidebooks and websites lacked in details, my mind more than made up for in expectations. Long before arriving in the country, I could picture myself at the closely-knit gathering, sipping steaming glasses of mint tea, connecting with new friends over the festival's fragrant namesake.

Liz met me in Tangier's Gare Tanger Ville station, where we bought tickets for our overnight train to Marrakech, stretched out our nearly six-foot frames across pumpkin-colored leather couchettes, and woke to fields separated by prickly pear cacti with a lone figure picking handfuls of grass at dawn. We were in Marrakech long enough to catch a bus 300 kilometers east to Kelaat M'Gouna, what we assumed, or rather hoped, was a small traditional village, its dusty air perhaps sweetened by the presence of roses. No doubt it would be a welcome contrast from Marrakech's crowd-jostling medinas and the twisting side streets of its *souks*.

The train had taken eleven hours, the bus would be six, but what propelled us, urging us ever forward, was our anticipation of the festival, an annual celebration to mark the rose harvest each spring.

We carry so much with us when we travel, much more than the neatly (or not so neatly) folded items in our suitcases. But the most dangerous thing we bring, tucked in between regulation-size shampoo bottles and extra pairs of socks, is expectation. The moment we begin to envision a new place, to believe how it will be, is the moment that same place begins to fail us.

In the title poem from her collection, *Questions of Travel,* Elizabeth Bishop writes, "Think of the long trip home. Should we have stayed at home and thought of here? Where should we be today? . . . Oh, must we dream our dreams and have them, too?"

Bishop perfectly captures the traveler's dilemma: Do we risk disappointment and failed hopes for the reality of somewhere different? Or would it not be better to leave our visions intact and live through imagination—not actual experience?

Such questions hovered uneasily in my mind as we set out from our guesthouse the first day of the festival. Crowds led us to a large amphitheater whose ring of concrete seats stretched several rows up. By ten in the morning, it was packed with flocks of young men perched on the top row, Berber women in their layers of crushed velvet and sequined chiffon, and men in colorful turbans and long white robes. Ice cream sellers with coolers hanging around their necks called out "*Hemeem, hemeem*" in high-pitched voices, the rose-flavored cream already dripping from children's chins and dancing down their arms like drops of rain on a window.

But there was no pageant this year as we'd read there would be, which meant no rose queen would be chosen either; all the handicrafts in the local market read "Made in China"; and the only roses we had yet to find were tightly furled buds that had been pierced by a needle, strung together in the shape of a heart and then hawked to tourists. Even Kelaat M'Gouna was far from the village we'd expected, its streets as clogged with festivalgoers and as difficult to navigate as Marrakech had been. Liz and I shifted from the amphitheater to the market and back again, both of us filling the space with chitchat, forever avoiding one word: disappointment.

"Let's go for a walk," Liz said. I suggested the city gate as a destination. We'd passed it on the bus ride in, two sets of imposing square pillars on either side of the road painted a bright-blush pink, but I hadn't been quick enough with my camera to get a shot of it. Now was my chance.

We left the festival behind, the tinny sounds of CD sellers' portable stereos slowly evaporating, the sun nearing its zenith above our heads. To our left, just beyond the town limits, dry, ochre hills rose away from us, appearing almost lunar with barely a few shrubs to break up the striated stone. To our right flowed the M'Goun River, feeding a lush riverbed of wheat fields, groves of olive, fig and almond trees, and, finally, endless hedges of luxuriant, fragrant rose bushes. For the first time all day, our steps leading us ever closer to the gate, I felt a sense of purpose for being here.

And that's when I saw her. It was her dress that caught my eye first, in the shade of blue I've always loved to call pavonine, after a vocab word from the sixth grade: *of or resembling the feathers of a peacock, as in coloring.* Although she was sitting in the shade of a billowing almond tree, perhaps 20 feet below the road in the sunken riverbed, she still shimmered, a few stray rays of sunlight dancing off the silky fabric that enclosed her.

She waved, as did the woman sitting next to her, a wave that soon became a beckoning, *come-hither* kind of gesture.

"Do you think she means us?" I asked Liz.

"Who else could it be?"

Liz was off before I had time to think, exchanging road for scrubby hillside, leaping with her long legs over a crevice in the ground. Tentatively, I followed suit and raced to catch up with her, curious about where this unexpected invitation might lead. We bowed our heads slightly beneath the low-hanging branches of the almond tree and joined them. The woman who'd waved first, the woman in pavonine blue, was named Hazo; the other was Arkaya, who was mysteriously introduced as Hazo's grand-mother's sister, despite how close in age they appeared. They motioned for us to sit beside them on two expansive blankets, where they reclined in dark headscarves, long dresses, and curiously colorful socks, with polka dot and striped patterns standing out from the rest of their clothing.

With her back resting against the tree, Arkaya sliced chunks of turnips, cauliflower, potatoes and onions onto her lap; Hazo sat across from us, bringing a metal pot to boil on a single gas burner and slipping in shards of sugar as large and pointed as daggers. She poured tea for all of us, teaching Liz and me how to say it in Darija—*atay*—but no matter how it was pronounced, tea had never tasted so sweet.

For the rest of the afternoon, we hardly moved from their sides. Their sons came later, as did Hazo's husband, a civil servant in a village 100 kilometers away. There were more introductions, more glasses of tea, and more Darija lessons. *Leghda* for lunch, *khala* for auntie, and—my favorite—*zween*. Beautiful. We tried to leave before lunch, hesitant to overstay our welcome, but the idea was quickly dismissed. After the vegetables had simmered long enough with thick pieces of lamb, the air fragrant with saffron, they were served in a single bowl in the middle of the blanket. Arkaya ripped bread into pieces, and we circled around the food, our shoulders pressing together.

"*Tch, tch!*" Hazo said. Eat, eat!

"Eat the meat!" her husband insisted, chiding us when we drifted too far from the dish.

I lost track of how many times I said *zween* about the meal.

When the last drop of juice had been soaked into bread, the blankets were cleared and Hazo and Arkaya lay down. Arkaya rested her head on Hazo's bent knees, and then motioned for me to do the same on hers. My eyes were closed and the breeze was soft, but I found comfort in more than our human nap chain; I was filled with the warmth of their kindness, with a hospitality I hadn't expected. I wondered when I would learn not to let my expectations get the best of me—and when I would remember that the most cherished memories from a place are so often the ones we didn't know to expect. We said goodbye, and Liz and I once again began making our way to the city gate.

Roses aren't supposed to let you down. And beneath an almond tree one afternoon in the Valley of Roses, they didn't.

Cradle

Clara Hsu

Africa,
we are locked in each other's consciousness.
You, vast, ancient, magnificent in blue
call me,
who long ago tumbled out of your bosom
into faraway lands.
Oozing the scent of exotica,
your messengers lead me
through labyrinthine trails.
I shed my skin
layers of translucent doldrums.
Your sequined dress billows
golden lips chant a lullaby

ochre arms enfold the first of my dreaming
take it back to a time
when I was very small.

What Price, Wisdom?

Christina Ammon

ABDUL GESTURED TO HEAVEN.

"I used to work for money. Now I work for Allah." We were sitting outside his ceramic shop in one of those rare beams of Moroccan sunlight that find their way into the Fez Medina at midday. Just a moment ago, he was laying on a heavy sales pitch for a ceramic *tagine*; now he was praising Allah.

I sipped my mint tea. This was not like shopping in America. The sales clerks at Victoria's Secret or The Gap are more interested in pushing three-for-the-price-of-two panties—or selling their credit line—than sitting in a ray of sunlight, drinking tea, and talking God.

But to be clear: Abdul *did* have a keen interest in selling this *tagine*. Anyone who has spent a split second in the Fez Medina knows that the shopkeepers are relentless. A chorus of "Just look!" and "Special price!" follows you everywhere you walk, and waiters trail you down the street waving menus touting *kefta* and couscous.

After tea, I bought the *tagine*—for too much money. Abdul hiked the price, but I hadn't the energy to protest. I placed it into my bag with the same resigned spirit that stuck me with a scarf I didn't need and a wooden toy top I never wanted (though it *did* have a spectacular spin).

The call to prayer sounded from a nearby mosque and I lumbered forth with my shopping bags. My hoard of overpriced gadgets was growing, but so was my collection of spiritual truths. It was hard to make sense of it. One minute Yousef Carpet Salesman was tricking me into his shop and the next, waxing on like Khalil Gibran.

The salesmen of the medina were shape-shifters.

Around the next corner it was Si Mohamud badgering me into his furniture shop. But soon enough the conversation turned to the weather. "One day sunny, one day raining. One day good, the next day bad." He stood in his *djellaba* among a collection of the antique vases. "That your heart is beating, this is important." He placed his hand on his chest. "Health. It is the only thing that matters."

Apparently, the shopkeepers aren't aware of the dirty secret of all thriving capitalist societies: Happy people don't buy things. Dissatisfaction—not gratitude—is what fuels consumerism: Tell them they are not thin enough, blonde enough, or young enough and their wallets will turn inside out. And lose the *Insha-Allah,* that laissez-faire sentiment that turns our fate over to the Higher Power. Tell them that with the right pair of skinny jeans, they can be the Masters of the Universe.

Later, earrings. "Enjoy every second. For you do not know when and where you will die," Rashid counseled as I leaned toward the mirror to inspect a pair of silver danglies and formulate my bid. My heart leapt and I plucked the earrings from my lobes. *What am I doing spending money in these dark shops when I should be out on the sunny rooftop, watching migrating storks and the springtime hills?*

On the way back to my *riad*, I realized that it's not just wise words that you find in the medina, but also wise postures. Between shop stalls, old men in *djellabas* leaned against weather-stained walls, content as horses turned out to pasture. They occupied sidewalk tables, taking in the scene over cups of mint tea that never seem to empty. Beyond the *souk* now, I passed the same plumber I passed every day, still resting in the same seat of repose in the same chair. Such postures don't exist in America. There, time is money, and everyone must fiddle with their cell phones, or be on their way somewhere. In the contented body-language of the Fassi lies a sort of somatic advertisement for Simply Being.

No shopping trip is perfunctory in the twisty byways of the medina. The sacred and the profane mix like intimate aromas, and aggressive sales pitches are in no way at odds with spiritual pursuits. False guides will bamboozle you into a tannery tour en-route to the mosque. Carpet sellers sing *Hamdulla!* and then rob you blind. The wisdom of the ages echoes off walls hung with overpriced kitsch. You set off scouting for a roll of toilet paper, and suddenly find yourself standing in the center of Si-Mohammed's antique shop, spellbound by his wisdom, and giving thanks for the very beating of your heart.

Mystery

I stand in a portico hung with gentian-blue ipomeas . . . and look out on a land of mists and mysteries; a land of trailing silver veils through which domes and minarets, mighty towers and ramparts of flushed stone, hot palm groves and Atlas snows, peer and disappear at the will of the Atlantic cloud drifts.

—Edith Wharton, *In Morocco*

I'brahim and Aisha

Clara Hsu

I'BRAHIM AND AISHA WENT into the Chigaga region of
the Sahara Desert with Youssef and two camels. Two days
before, it had rained. The sandy floor had turned into a mud
plain. The sun baked the earth into clay and the thin brittle
surfaces cracked under their feet. Youssef in his black turban,
light-blue, long tunic with gold nomadic emblem walked in a
relaxed manner, leading the camels on a leash. He told I'brahim
and Aisha to walk in the camel's shadows so they wouldn't be
scorched by the sun. I'brahim put on a dark-blue turban, the
color of nomads'. It covered his head and face, exposing only
his large eyeglasses. Aisha draped her head with a yellow
turban, the color of the sun. She trailed behind her companions
with her dainty steps.

Hours and hours they walked, crossing deserts of black and blue stones, crossing dry riverbeds covered in small shrubs and fossil rocks, crossing rippling sand dunes. Youssef made lunch under an acacia tree: a Berber salad of tomatoes, onions, green peppers and cucumbers with sardine; and a pot of cumin chicken with plenty of sauce. I'brahim and Aisha rested on long mats in the shadow of the tree and drank strong sugary green tea. They were too tired to move. While they napped, Youssef washed all the dishes and packed them away.

On and on they walked. Aisha's delicate ankles began to hurt. She didn't complain but Youssef wisely put her on the camel. Aisha could see from the hump the camel's small, fuzzy brown ears sticking out. His long neck curved downward and up, rotating at the end as his powerful thighs moved back and forth.

At night they made camp on the sand. Aisha and I'brahim gathered dried sticks and made a small fire. Youssef sang and played drum on a large, green water can.

"Dance, Aisha!" He commanded.

Aisha, barefoot in her white *djellaba* with black thin stripes got up and danced, clapping her hands to the drum beat, lifting her head to the stars. I'brahim pulled out his mini recorder and stopped the show.

"Ok. Start again," he said after he pushed the "record" button.

That night Aisha saw the moon three times, each at a different angle as she slept and woke. I'brahim woke to the gurgling sounds of the camels and found them sitting in the sand, facing each other, rubbing necks.

Youssef opened his eyes as soon as he heard Aisha stirring beside him. He got up and started to boil water for tea and coffee. There were bread and jam and soft cheese for breakfast, peppered with a little sand.

The sky was bright blue, and the sun rose rapidly. After swishing Listerine in his mouth, I'brahim took off his clothes. His skin was pale as the dawning sand. He changed into a pure white, long shirt down to his ankles. As he walked his white shirt shimmered against the dunes, now deepening into gold as the sun intensified. I'brahim's form fluttered in the breeze as he trailed behind Youssef. Aisha sitting high on the camel wound the turban around her head and covered her face. The sun impressed itself on her nose, turning it red. Her black hair felt wiry and sandy. She waved her hand in front of her eyes. Flies flew up and landed back on her yellow turban. From a distance I'brahim thought they looked like raisins.

They walked much of the day, stopping to make a Berber omelet with onions, tomatoes and cumin; and lots of strong tea. Aisha was most happy in the evening, after the grueling day, to sit on top of the dune and gaze at the stars. She thought of her children and wrote their names on the sand. A shooting star brought her wishes to her faraway home.

They slept in a tent because it was cold and windy. Aisha slept between Youssef and I'brahim. Three bodies each covered under heavy and sandy blankets. She felt Youssef's restlessness, grunting and turning in the night.

On the last day Youssef took Aisha's hand and walked with her. Youssef's legs were lean and powerful. His feet were thick and every toe was muscular. Aisha counted; they were walking three paces to a second. Her breaths became heavy as she stumbled up the sand dunes. Youssef held her hand firmly, tugging her arm to his side. After a short time Aisha's throat was parched and she could hear her heartbeats in her ears. Youssef put her back on the camel.

I'brahim was delighted to find a herd of goats after they crossed the Zagora River. He walked with the shepherds until they arrived at M'hamid, their destination desert town. Aisha stood in a mud path between houses and watched the camels being unloaded. A few girls who were playing jump rope down the path ran over to Aisha. When she uncovered her face they kept staring at her. Aisha opened her backpack and took out a candy. She gave it to the girl nearest her. Suddenly many children ran out of the mud houses, their hands outstretched, circling around Aisha.

"*Bon Bon, Bon Bon,*" they cried.

After Aisha handed out all her candy, she went into a mud house with I'brahim and Youssef. There, friends awaited them and they had lunch together sitting on the carpeted floor around a low table. Before they left, I'brahim and Aisha gave Youssef big hugs and thanked the camels. They took off their turbans and resumed their former personas.

The Blind Guides of the Sahara

Phil Cousineau

IN 1815, A CARAVAN OF TWO thousand camels vanished
without a trace on the old merchant route from Timbuktu
to Morocco. The fear that followed gave rise to a search for
preternaturally talented guides to lead caravans through the
Sahara, the Lands of Fear and Lands of Terror. The legend goes
that a small band of blind Berbers appeared one day who could
navigate the desert by the smells of the sand and the sounds of
the wind.

A host of travel legends stream through my mind one
afternoon when I find myself lost in the maze of the bazaar in
Marrakech. I stop at the stall of a brass and silver artisan to
ask for directions back to the marketplace of Jamaa el Fna, and
am so grateful I buy a small vase for my sister, Nicole. When I
hand a fifty-*dirham* note to the old vendor in the white spiral of
turban, he tenderly touches it to his forehead and kisses it. With

the hesitation of a poor man, he takes out the only ten-*dirham* note left in his leather pouch, unfolds it like a prayer rug, and hands it over to me so desolately I feel guilty for taking my change.

I nod respectfully, then move on, drifting through the labyrinthine world of chaffering merchants hawking their silks, Turkish rugs, spices, aphrodisiacs, sponges, lacquered boxes, scarves, and robes for desert travelers.

Everywhere I walk around the bazaar I am followed by beggars and orphans. I cannot elude them, no matter what I say or how fast I try to run away. *"Un stylo, monsieur, je vais à l'école, je n'ai pas un stylo . . . ,"* they cry. *"Je n'ai rien, monsieur. . . .* Gentle souvenirs? Kind gifts? Cheap, special price for you, Joe."

I push on through the densely crowded bazaar, past touts and barkers. Women are lying over the thresholds of their homes, arms and legs splayed wide, as they're being tattooed by their servants on their hands and feet with rooster-red henna for an upcoming festival. Further on, a raccoon-eyed thief is chased by two shopkeepers flashing knives at him. A German tour group barters aggressively at the door of a Persian rug shop whose owner is not amused. A foreign journalist tugs at his meerschaum pipe in an old teahouse.

On the way back to my hotel in the late afternoon, I pause to marvel at the way the sun is raking through the slatted rooftops of the bazaar. Twilight is approaching: "the swift hour," as Bedouins call it. A coral sunset silhouettes the minarets that crackle with the pious voice of the *muezzin*. The prayers of the faithful mix with the smoke from hundreds of food stands and rise entwined into the sweltering sky. White-robed merchants disappear down the dark passages of the souks, replaced by acrobats, dancers, snake charmers, water carriers, spice traders, booksellers, glad-handing tour guides, and skittish tourists.

I make my way through the human maelstrom, pause near a tea stand. Using his forefinger, a berobed storyteller draws a circle in the dirt around him, leaving a small opening. He then beckons a group of Berber musicians to step inside the circle to accompany his sand-rubbed legends. Only when they are seated does the storyteller bend down and close the circle with his finger.

I'm transfixed. An hour passes, then another. It's dark, but for torches and gaslights, when I notice I've been followed by a handsome young man in blue jeans and Sorbonne T-shirt. He has the charming world-weariness of a young Omar Sharif. In the old reflex of the hounded traveler, I turn to go, and he grasps my arm and murmurs, "I am Zachariah. I would like to lead you through the medina."

I wave him away and head back to my hotel, but he persists, following me through the next eleven twists of the maze of lookalike alleyways. In contrast to the hustle lines I've heard all day, he appears elegantly subdued as he describes his father's work in the Marrakech schools, and his brother's job in France.

On the next turn, he stops, looks around for unwanted stragglers, and grabs the iron lion's head doorknocker of a heavy oak door. He knocks firmly twice and, with a graceful wave of his arm, beckons me inside his family's house. I hesitate, tugging at my earlobe, as I do when I can't make up my mind. Nervously, I look up and down the now empty lanes of the medina. He tempts me by opening the medieval door just enough to allow me to see a blue-tiled oasis of softly bubbling fountains, bamboo bird cages, lemon and orange trees, and to hear the sweet sounds of Berber folk music on an old radio. Despite my skepticism that he's just another hustler, I'm fairly charmed and open to an adventure.

No risk, no story.

I follow him inside, immediately cooled by the gentle breeze inside the courtyard.

"You must help me, my kind American friend," he says before imperiously snapping his fingers at a young cinnamon-skinned servant. She bows and scurries off for the requisite mint tea.

"What do you mean *must* help you?" I ask, not sure if I want to hear the answer. It's uncomfortably quiet while we wait for the servant. "I don't understand."

"I am nothing here, there is nothing here for me," Zachariah says sadly. "I once dreamed of Paris, but my brother and my cousins there tell me of terrible racism toward Moroccans. It is no home for us. *C'est trop dangereux.*"

Finally the servant arrives with the tea service, bows and disappears quickly. Like a fool, I try to explain how difficult it is to immigrate to America, that we have our own problems at home, just as serious, only different. He cringes like a cosseted soul suddenly afraid of being on his own, then waves me off dismissively.

Sternly, he orders the maid to bring us a brass platter of sweets. Without missing a beat of his pitch for exile to America, he brings out the family photo album. As if on cue, his mother, his sister, his grandmother all arrive, to prove his excellent stock, or prove he would be a good investment for me back home.

I thank him for each round of tea and the wedges of honey and walnut pastry and the family introductions, but resolutely keep trying to dissuade him. I startle myself with my argument against emigration, my sobering tales of unemployment statistics, outrageously expensive colleges, crime in the street. But he doesn't hear a word I say.

"I will sleep on your floor; I will cook for you, clean for you." He's so dazed by California Dreamin' he won't stand for any myth-busting tales. "You won't even know I'm there," he says plaintively. "I want to improve myself. America is my last hope."

Seeing how utterly unconvinced I am, he turns on me, accusing me of being ungrateful for the hospitality he's shown and, worse, of American superiority. "Do you not think me good enough for your world?"

"No," I say, feeling claustrophobic. "I just don't believe it's what you're looking for." Yet, as the words dribble out, I'm unsure of what I'm saying.

"What do you think I'm looking for?" he asks peevishly.

The servant returns with another brass platter of tea and Turkish sweets. He curtly waves her away.

"I don't know," I admit. "Let's just say it's a very lonely place for people a long way from home."

There is also a good chance he thinks I'm just a traveling fool, impervious to the obvious glories of my own country.

Suddenly, our little party is over. He stands up, snapping his fingers imperiously, and leads me back through the blue-tiled courtyard, past the fruit trees arching over the fountain, past the giggling servants, who bow gracefully, their hands over their mouths, past his family, who are now smiling woodenly. In the curling shadows of the medieval wooden door that leads back out into the kasbah, with the heat of the medina and the desert pouring through the crack in the door, he grips my hand, slipping me his father's Old World calling card.

In a steely voice, he whispers, "Don't forget what I've done for you. Don't forget me. Write to me in care of my father's school." Pausing, as if reading the scroll of his future in the afternoon air, he says, *My life is in your hands."*

I give him my address. We stand there for a few moments, awkwardly shaking hands, neither one of us willing to lose face by letting go first. The smell of orange trees fills my head like a spell. I inhale like a man who's found the path to bliss. I drink in with my eyes the arabesque patterns of the blue tiles on the walls around us. They seem to glow from within and put me into a mild trance. I don't want to leave; he doesn't want to let go. For me this is the enchanted world—for him a nightmare. I think of the blind guides of the desert making their way through the vast unknown by the genius of their keen noses and lush faith, and wonder whether Zachariah will find the guide he needs to make his way to his true home.

Old carts clatter on the cobbles beyond the thick medieval door. He is sullenly silent when I say thank you and goodbye, and good luck and, yes, I'll reply to you if you write to me.

He has stopped hearing. Something he can't yet describe is lurking inside him, seeking another kind of guide, a different way through the mirage that is his dream of escape, not mine.

I can still taste the honey and walnuts. How can that be?

And so the legend caravans on.

To See the Sounds of Magic

Anna Elkins

The Islamic holy city of Moulay Idriss, Morocco

Our guide's name is Magic.
Or, I thought it was until I asked
him to write it for me—*Majid*.
Between the legends he tells
of *djinns* and double doors,
Majid listens to our questions
and leads us through his streets.
He turns a whitewashed corner
and stops, looking over a cliff.
We gather near, waiting for the next
marvel-fact of this ageless place.
He says nothing, just stares out.
We follow his steady eyes and gasp—

there, across a valley we didn't know
we'd ascended from,
glows the domed hill of the city
in fading sunlight, flanked by
green fields, green mountains.
The soul is rich here," Majid says,
in his thick accent.
Only he didn't say that. He said *soil,*
but it took me a moment of context—
olive orchards, vineyards—
to hear what he meant.
We just visited a bakery—saw
and heard how bakers transform grains.
Tomorrow, we visit a vineyard—will see
and hear how vintners transform grapes.
But right now, we stand before the
last light of day, our selves transforming.
"We watched the sun set," we say later.
But we didn't.
We heard it—donkey bray,
call to prayer, swallow song.
We heard it—the sound of our
own souls growing,
even if we couldn't see them.
Like magic.

Timelessness

But I come from no country, from no city, no tribe. I am the son of the road, my country is the caravan, my life the most unexpected of voyages.

—Amin Mallouf, *Leo Africanus*

The Marrakech Way

Phil Cousineau

DEEP IN THE THROBBING HEART of the covered bazaar, the last of the weary shopkeepers are closing their doors for Ramadan. The dusty maze of streets is so quiet I can hear the shuffle of my own sandals. Near the Jamaa el Fna plaza, I find four blind drum-makers on a bench next to the door of an old music shop. They are shadow-striped by the afternoon light coming in through the slatted roof of the market, which intensifies the thrilling shadowplay of their music. One man plays a wooden flute, another a slender-necked *rebec*, a third shakes a jangly tambourine, and the fourth thrums a goatskin drum. All while singing folk songs as old as the desert. Their self-assured smiles are strong enough to prop up the crumbling walls of the medina. The oldest musician is a Bedouin nomad with a dusty beard and a rhythm that sounds like an approaching sandstorm. His head sways back and forth, in and out of the slanting light, as if he's listening to the bells of a distant caravan juddering across the desert. He gestures for me to come out of the shadows. I lean down to hear him.

"With hands, is Marrakech way," he says softly. "No feeling with sticks. Just with hands comes feeling, for drumming."

His own sun-burnished hands dance over the taut drum skin as if they're circling God. His voice yearns, finds Him. Higher and higher he pushes the prayer high into the impossibly blue skies above the towering red walls of the city. Smiling, he invites me to join them for some moist wild figs and glasses of tea with floating mint sprigs.

"And you, kind sir," he asks, pouring the steaming tea for me in a long graceful arc. "What do you feel, with your hands?"

One, two, three sugar cubes fall into the hot glass, splashing in the hot tea, and dissolving bead by bead.

"What is your way through the world, for feeling?" he asks.

My hands wind tight around the glass, absorbing the heat. The sugar vanishes, becoming indistinguishable from the tea.

Far below me, below the cool sand, below the ancient city, below the fossils laid down long ago, a rumble begins. It is the sound of words said long ago, prayers lifted from a very great distance, and now knocking on the door of my heart, waiting for an answer that needs more music.

Desire

Siddharth Gupta

Winds hide

Winds reveal

The desert is only a keeper

Indifferent.

But what it holds cannot be denied.

We who seek its secrets,

Are destined to be buried amongst them.

Baptism of Solitude[4]

Paul Bowles

IMMEDIATELY WHEN YOU ARRIVE in Sahara, for the first or the tenth time, you notice the stillness. An incredible, absolute silence prevails outside the towns; and within, even in busy places like the markets, there is a hushed quality in the air, as if the quiet were a conscious force which, resenting the intrusion of sound, minimizes and disperses sound straightaway. Then there is the sky, compared to which all other skies seem faint-hearted efforts. Solid and luminous, it is always the focal point of the landscape. At sunset, the precise, curved shadow of the earth rises into it swiftly from the horizon, cutting into light section and dark section. When all daylight is gone, and the space is thick with stars, it is still of an intense and burning

4   Paul Bowles, "The Secret Sahara" ("Baptism of Solitude"), January, 1953, *Travels: Collected Writings, 1950-1993*

blue, darkest directly overhead and paling toward the earth, so that the night never really goes dark.

You leave the gate of the fort or town behind, pass the camels lying outside, go up into the dunes, or out onto the hard, stony plain and stand awhile alone. Presently, you will either shiver and hurry back inside the walls, or you will go on standing there and let something very peculiar happen to you, something that everyone who lives there has undergone and which the French call *le baptême de solitude.* It is a unique sensation, and it has nothing to do with loneliness, for loneliness presupposes memory. Here in this wholly mineral landscape lighted by stars like flares, even memory disappears; nothing is left but your own breathing and the sound of your heart beating. A strange, and by no means pleasant, process of reintegration begins inside you, and you have the choice of fighting against it, and insisting on remaining the person you have always been, or letting it take its course. For no one who has stayed in the Sahara for a while is quite the same as when he came. . . . Perhaps the logical question to ask at this point is: Why go? The answer is that when a man has been there and undergone the baptism of solitude he can't help himself. Once he has been under the spell of the vast luminous, silent country, no other place is quite strong enough for him, no other surroundings can provide the supremely satisfying sensation of existing in the midst of something that is absolute. He will go back, whatever the cost in time or money, for the absolute has no price.

Afterword

Erin Byrne

THE ANCIENT STORYTELLER OF MOROCCO

THE CREASES ON THE MAN'S forehead are shadowed in the firelight but the skin over his cheekbones is smooth, the color of caramel. He begins to speak in the language of his own Berber tribe, sounds rolling up through his throat. He punctuates the end of his sentences sharply and lifts his chin for emphasis. When he leans forward on his cane his cape flurries, then settles on his shoulders.

"*Lahalaho Khair!*" He booms as his eyes mirror sparks that spray from the fire. All might be good. He is telling the story of a king whose advisor repeats this phrase even in the midst of disaster.

The storyteller raises his hands, one clutching the cane, in a wide arc, and the colors of his cloak flash: scarlet, cobalt, saffron, green. His eyebrows dart together: The king is angry. He growls and points: The advisor is sent away.

It is the year 400 BC. On this dark night, through a canopy of sky, stars illuminate the undulating hills of the Middle Atlas

Mountains. In a wide, flat area, a group of people are circled, their attention riveted to this man, the keeper of legends, the teller of tales of lessons learned in humility, loyalty, generosity, and love. Different tribes have recently joined together to form the kingdom of Mauritania; now they are one and they look to him to create a common history.

—◦◦◦—

The storyteller took my hand and offered both cheeks, smooth under my lips. In the year 2015, he had been telling stories for fifty-six years or over two thousand, depending upon one's belief in reincarnation.

"*Metsherrfin,*" I said, "pleased to meet you" in Darija, I thought; just in case I added, "*Enchantée.*"

Ahmed Ezzarghani, called Hajj, which means pilgrim, or one who has gone to Mecca, smiled and nodded. He was wearing one yellow scarf around his head, another around his neck, and a midnight-blue cape over a cream-colored *djellaba*. His face was chiseled, handsome.

I asked the translator, Amine, a bright-eyed, bearded youth who wore a baseball cap and a flannel shirt, to ask Hajj if he would teach me to tell stories.

I myself came to Morocco to teach a storytelling workshop to writers, but in the flash of a second—or thousands of years— my expertise vanished.

As a young historian in 1959, Hajj was captivated by *One Thousand and One Nights*, and began to travel around Morocco picking up stories. In Moroccan tradition, the story is like a song, with writer, composer, and musicians all adding their own individual flair. The teller is the singer who, as Billie Holiday, Michael Bublé and countless others did with Sinatra's songs, creates his own version. In this way, Hajj made the stories his own, and developed a repertoire of sixty to seventy tales.

"The way you say it and the way you move reveal your own way, your own emotion," Hajj later told our group through Amine's eyebrow-punctuated translations.

Moroccan stories can last days, weeks, months, and Hajj continued to spin them. He married and settled in Fez, but traveled away from home to perform, to hide his trade, as story-telling was not a prestigious occupation, earning precious few *dirhams*. One day after hawking his watch to get to Casablanca, he spied his wife's uncle in the audience, and was "outed," but the uncle was charmed. Hajj then moved to Marrakech.

Moroccan stories, told in third person, evoke specific moral lessons. The focus is not the teller but the tale, which is chosen and adjusted to suit the audience.

For decades, Hajj spun these stories with wide gestures and flourishes in Jamaa el Fna, the island of chaos that is the Marrakech square, but eventually more touristic offerings crowded him out. Snake charmers swayed, musicians played, fortune-tellers brayed, and sellers hawked their wares, driving out the traditional storytellers, now in danger of extinction.

Hajj, one of the few remaining *Hakawati*, master story-tellers, has been featured on Al Jazeera and invited to work with professors and experts from all over the world, even done a TEDx talk. He is passing his torch to vibrant young apprentices like Amine, who enjoys headbanging metal and is active in "Maroc Jeunes" social and cultural club, and Malika, a pretty young woman who wears jeans and savvy boots and tells stories in a perky, expressive style.

We were gathered at Café Clock, Marrakech, a beehive of a hangout that climbs three stories to a rooftop terrace. Mike Richardson offered this space as an alternative to Jemaa el Fna[5], and the place has become a treasure chest in which to preserve this ancient art. Twice weekly, crowds gather here to listen and learn.

That first evening, after a feast of camel burgers and *kefta* kebabs, Amine and Malika told stories in English, Amine's about a blacksmith and a judge's daughter, and Malika's about a man whose obsession with winning the heart of a woman drove him to extremes.

Then Hajj arose, his robes swishing, his eyes burning, and began speaking in a voice that rolled like an exotic earthquake, waving his cane and thumping it to the floor. He scowled, he grimaced, he exploded with laughter. When I had met him hours earlier, he'd seemed aware of his prestige but now his ego had retreated and in its place was pure *story,* underneath which, as if through a clear river, were the emotions we all feel. I was mesmerized and leaned forward so as not to miss a syllable.

It did not matter that he spoke in Darija and I didn't comprehend a word: I *understood.*

---

5   In Café Clock in Fez, Hajj's old friend Mokliss vibrates with his own enthusiastic band of apprentices, whom we would meet later in the week.

Our group of writers spent ten days with these three, traveling from Marrakech to Moulay Idriss. I was there as co-instructor, but became a student, wishing only to learn from these gifted performers and to encourage the other writers to absorb their magic.

Hajj seemed to be woven of the ancient *and* the modern. He embodied stories the Berbers told centuries ago, and looked the picture of a traditional Moroccan *Hakawati*, but often pulled his phone out of the pocket of his robes and huddled over it; or sat down on a step and leaned forward, elbows on knees, dragging on a cigarette like the Moroccan Marlboro Man while teasing my co-instructor Doug about being *shebe* (white-haired); or whipped out his Kindle to read a line or two. But when Hajj told a story, time and distance morphed and language was transcended.

Malika took me under her wing, telling me that Moroccan stories were often about kings and thieves and plots, and always held a deeper meaning, with an essential ingredient: "Moroccans will never accept the moral without humor," she said, as if referring to a glass of tea crammed with mint leaves and spoonfuls of sugar. Her grandmother had told stories until she died at 108 years old and when Malika began working with Hajj, she recognized just how many stories they had in common. While her grandmother told her tales behind the closed doors of home, Malika performs hers in public. She told me someone once asked Hajj how many stories he had and he replied: "From my head to my feet."

Malika told me that learning these stories has changed her; she treats people differently.

"Hajj has chosen this story for you to learn," she said one day, as we sat at a table in the square of Moulay Idriss, sipping cappuccinos among the crowd of mostly men.

The story, *Lahalaho Khair,* is about a king's minister who is also his friend, who, no matter what happens, insists that things might turn out well. When disaster strikes, this lands him in jail, but through a series of events, the king comes to see that the minister saved his life, and his claim that "all might be good" was true all along.

I told it at Café Clock, trying to tap into the flow of story as Hajj had.

Lahalaho Khair is a story that, since that week, I've repeatedly replayed in my mind. I have found that this gem of a phrase holds a kernel of eternal wisdom, and have come to believe that it is this that makes stories last.

"*Lahalaho Khair,*" I now chant to myself when the going gets rough, when a decision must be made, or events seem to implode. *All might be good, all might be good, all might be good* has become my mantra. But the last time I told the story, the meaning of it underwent a kind of alchemy.

One night in November, soon after the Moroccan trip, I hosted a salon in Paris with the theme of storytelling. Eighteen people gathered, five of whom had been on the Moroccan trip, and we told our stories, and shared photos and memories of Hajj, Amine and Malika. It was a dazzling evening, a celebration.

After most of the guests had departed, a latecomer burst in with the news that something was happening out in the city. He strode to the window and opened it. We heard the wail of what sounded like a thousand and one sirens.

All through the tenuous weeks after the terrorist attacks, I noticed good cropping up all over Paris: a piano set up outside Bataclan where two men filled the air with melancholy beauty, people honoring their departed loved ones with dignity, quiet kindnesses and the nurturing of wounded spirits. All of it mingled with my Darija phrase to fan a tiny flame of hope inside of me.

I thought of something Hajj had said. "The more stories you hear, the more you learn about life. Then you know how to live."

———◦◦◦———

If you dig deep enough, you reach the universal emotion, as the ancient storyteller of Morocco illustrated so clearly for me, and it seems to me that the writers included in this collection did just that. In this world of wars and anger and uncertainties and rifts, such stories endure. Each story in *Vignettes & Postcards from Morocco* reflects humanity's common values in a different way, from experiencing memories of a deceased beloved to pondering the roots of one's own name, from a family bonding over a simple meal to a man born anew in the timeless sands of the Sahara.

If these tales of quests and of mysteries, of traditions and memory and wisdom have led you to explore your own stories, have piqued your curiosity, consoled you, bolstered you, or given you a glimmer of how to live, then I think Hajj would lift his chin, his cape fluttering a little, fix his shining eyes on you and say, "*Lahalaho Khair.*"

Glossary

Glossary of a few Moroccan words . . .

Adhan: The Muslim call to prayer, traditionally called over a loudspeaker from the mosque, five times a day.

Atlas Mountains: A mountain range that stretches across northwestern Africa through Algeria, Morocco and Tunisia.

Berber: All-encompassing name for the native, pre-Arab inhabitants of North Africa and their descendents. Also known as "Amazigh" or in plural, "Imazighen," Berbers are traditionally a nomadic culture. Berber also refers to the variety of languages spoken by the Berber people.

Babouches: Slippers with no heel

Dar: House.

Darija: Moroccan Arabic.

Dirham: Moroccan currency.

Djellaba (Djellabah/Jellaba): Traditional Berber robe/cloak–loose-fitting, hooded, and made of wool or (in modern days) cotton.

Fakir: An educated man.

Fassi: Inhabitant of Fez.

Hammam: Turkish-style bathhouse, similar to ancient Roman baths, steam baths and saunas. Traditionally communal, hammams are typically separated by gender and contain a series of treatment rooms—including steam, massage, and cold baths. Modern hammams range from simple communal bathing spots to luxury spas.

Imam: Head of the Muslim community. The title is also used in the Koran to refer to leaders and to Abraham.

Inshallah: God willing.

Jinn (Jann/Djinn): Supernatural creatures in Islamic mythology.

Koran/ Qur'an: Islamic Holy Text.

Maghreb: Literally "west" in Arabic, Maghreb refers to the region of North Africa bordering the Mediterranean Sea.

Medina: Literally "city" in Arabic, medina today refers to the ancient walled city—often made up of maze-like series of narrow passages.

Muezzin: The mosque official who calls Muslims to prayer.

Riad: House or palace with a central, interior, open-sky courtyard or garden.

Rif (Riff): Area of northeastern Morocco made up of mountains, fields and desert, traditionally inhabited Berbers. The name Rif is also used to describe Rif-dwellers.

Salaam Aleikum: Greeting. Peace be with you. (The response, Aleikum Salaam: With you be peace.)

Souk (Souq): An open-air marketplace or bazaar.

Sufi: A religious mystic in the Islamic tradition.

Tagine: Traditional North African stew typically of meat, vegetables and sometimes fruit. Widely popular in Morocco, tagines are classically slow-cooked, outdoors over hot coals throughout the day. This classic stew takes its name, literally, from the special ceramic, dome-like dish its cooked and served in.

Zellij: Terra cotta tilework covered with enamel.

Biographical Notes

Erin Byrne writes travel essays, poetry, fiction and screenplays. Her work has won numerous awards including three Grand Prize Solas Awards for Travel Story of the Year, the Readers' Favorite Award, Foreword Reviews Book of the Year Finalist, and an Accolade Award for film. She is the author of *Wings: Gifts of Art, Life, and Travel in France* (Travelers' Tales, 2016), and editor of the *Vignettes & Postcards* series. Erin's screenplay, *Siesta*, is in pre-production in Spain, and she is writer of *The Storykeeper*, an award-winning film about occupied Paris. She is an occasional guest instructor at Shakespeare and Company Bookstore in Paris, and teaches on Deep Travel trips. Erin is currently working on a novel series, *The Storykeeper of Paris*. www.e-byrne.com.

Photographers and Artists:

Omar Chennafi is a talented and charismatic presence in the Fez Medina. He is a photographer for the Ministry of Tourism and has been official photographer of The Sacred Music Festival in Fez. His photos have appeared in many publications, including *Time* magazine. Chennafi's work deftly mediates two perspectives: that of the tourists who treasure the medina as a UNESCO World Heritage Site and the perspective of residents who often view it as a slum. Chennafi bridges these two worlds with his images.

Siddharth Gupta is a photographer and storyteller currently based out of Mumbai, India. He completed his masters in literature from the University of Delhi, and a masters in filmmaking from the New York Film Academy. His short film *No Vacancy* was selected as a part of the prestigious Cannes Film Festival in 2012 and his photography work has been exhibited in New York and Los Angeles. Deeply fascinated by all forms of storytelling, written, visual, oral and physical (dance), Siddharth travels around the globe telling stories, learning languages and creating worlds made out of words and pictures.

Anna Elkins is a traveling poet and painter. She earned a BA in art and English and an MFA and Fulbright Fellowship in poetry. Her writings have been published in journals and books, and her paintings hang on walls around the world. She has written, painted, and taught on six continents. She is the author of the illustrated vignette, *The Heart Takes Flight,* the novel *The Honeylicker Angel,* and the poetry collection *The Space Between.* Anna is illustrator of *Wings* by Erin Byrne. She sets up her easel and writing desk in the mythical State of Jefferson. www.annaelkins.com

CONTRIBUTORS:

Amy Gigi Alexander is a traveler, explorer, and travel writer who also writes fiction and memoir. Once she decided to become a writer and give herself totally to the craft, her writing life bloomed. Her work crosses genres and blends her own history with classic narratives and magical realism. She writes for many international newspapers, magazines and websites and is featured in multiple anthologies of both personal essays and travelogues. She has several books in progress, and the first will be published in 2016. She shares long form stories, interviews, and inspirations about the power of goodness on her website, www.amygigialexander.com while she divides her time between the United States, France, and Mexico.

Lisa Alpine is the author of *Wild Life: Travel Adventures of a Worldly Woman* (Foreword Reviews' Gold Medal winner INDIEFAB Book of the Year Award and Best Travel Book 2014 North American Book Awards) and *Exotic Life: Travel Tales*

of an Adventurous Woman (1st place North American Book Awards). Her story *Fish Trader Ray* won the Solas Award silver medal for Best Travel Story of the Year—included in *Wild Life* and Travelers' Tales *Best Travel Writing Vol. #10*. Lisa hosts the "Adventure Travel Stories with an All-Star Cast" literary series at the Mill Valley Library and Book Passage. She resides in Mill Valley, California, and the Big Island of Hawai'i.

Leyla Giray Alyanak was born in Paris and raised around the world. She is a former foreign correspondent with a passion for travel and improving people's lives in developing countries. At forty-three she decided to travel the world solo for six months. She was gone three years, finding time to get lost in a Mozambican minefield, paddle out of a flood in the Philippines, and get stampeded by an elephant cow in Nigeria. Leyla works for an international development agency in Geneva. Her book, *Women on the Road,* shows women over forty how to plan and take the trip of their dreams.

Christina Ammon has penned stories on a wide range of topics, from flying with raptors in Nepal to exploring the underground wine scene in Morocco. She received the Oregon Literary Arts Fellowship for Creative Nonfiction, and her articles and photos have appeared in *Conde Nast, Hemispheres, The San Francisco Chronicle, The L.A. Times, The Oregonian* and many other publications. www.vanabonds.com.

Paul Bowles was born in Queens, New York in 1910. In 1930 he visited Morocco for the first time, with Aaron Copland, with whom he was studying music. His early reputation was as a composer and he wrote the scores for several Tennessee Williams plays. Bowles married the writer Jane Auer in 1938, and after the war the couple settled in Tangier. In Morocco, Bowles turned principally to fiction. *The Sheltering Sky*— inspired by his travels in the Sahara—was a *New York Times* bestseller in 1950, and has gone on to sell more than 250,000 copies. It was followed by three further novels, numerous short stories, nonfiction, and translations. Bowles died in Tangier in 1999.

Michael Chabon's novel *The Amazing Adventures of Kavalier & Clay* won the New York Society Library Prize for Fiction, the Bay Area Book Reviewers Award, the Commonwealth Club Gold Medal, and the Pulitzer Prize. His novella *The Final Solution* (2004) was awarded the 2005 National Jewish Book Award and also the 2003 Aga Khan Prize for Fiction by *The Paris Review*. Michael Chabon is the chairman of the board of directors at the MacDowell Colony and a member of the American Academy of Arts and Letters.

Suzanna Clarke is the author of *A House in Fez*, which chronicles her journey to restore an ancient *riad* in the heart of the Fez Medina. Clarke has worked as a photographer, feature writer, and arts editor for *The Courier-Mail* in Brisbane, Australia. She and her husband Sandy McCutcheon now live in the medina. They run the English language blog on Morocco, *The View from Fez*, and use the income from it for community charity projects.

Phil Cousineau is a freelance writer, documentary filmmaker, and creativity consultant. His thirty-plus published works include bestsellers *The Art of Pilgrimage*, *The Book of Roads*, *The Hero's Journey: the Life and Work of Joseph Campbell*, and *Stoking the Creative Fires*. Recent books include T*he Art of Travel Journal*, and *Burning the Midnight Oil*. Cousineau also has twenty documentary film credits including *The Hero's Journey: The Life and Work of Joseph Campbell*, *Wayfinders: A Pacific Odyssey*, and the Academy Award-nominated *Forever Activists: Stories from the Abraham Lincoln Brigade*. Since 2009, Cousineau has been host of "Global Spirit," on PBS and Link TV, and is currently a guest host on "New Dimensions Radio."

Sabrina Crawford hails from the as-yet-undead hinterlands of newspapers and magazines. An award-winning feature writer and arts and culture critic, she's interviewed everyone from former Rep. Tom Lantos to Guns N' Roses guitar god, Slash, amassing a rare fortune in random facts. Her illustrious credits include: staff writer for *The San Francisco Examiner*, A&E critic for *The San Francisco Bay Guardian*, associate editor of *DRUM!* magazine, researcher at *Wired* and author of *The Newcomer's Handbook for the San Francisco Bay Area*. Currently she's working on a book about literary salons, writing essays, teaching and trying (often laughably) to master Italian and French.

Marcia DeSanctis is the *New York Times* bestselling author of *100 Places in France Every Woman Should Go* (Travelers' Tales, 2014). She is a former television news producer who has worked for Barbara Walters, ABC, CBS, and NBC News. Her work has appeared in *Vogue, Marie Claire, Town & Country, O the Oprah Magazine, National Geographic Traveler, More, Tin House,* and *The New York Times,* and other publications. She is the recipient of four Lowell Thomas Awards for excellence in travel journalism, including one for Travel Journalist of the Year for her essays from Rwanda, Haiti, France and Russia.

James Michael Dorsey is an explorer, author, and lecturer who has spent two decades researching remote cultures worldwide. He is a contributing editor at *Transitions Abroad* and frequent contributor to *United Airlines* magazine. He has written for *Colliers, The Christian Science Monitor, Los Angeles Times, BBC Wildlife,* and *Perceptive Travel.* He is a foreign correspondent for *Camerapix International* and a travel consultant to Brown & Hudson of London. His latest book, *Vanishing Tales From Ancient Trails* was published in April, 2015. His work is included in many travel anthologies, including *Best Travel Writing, Volume 10.* James is a fellow of the Explorers Club. www.jamesdorsey.com

Darrin DuFord is the author of *Is There a Hole in the Boat? Tales of Travel in Panama without a Car,* silver medalist in the 2007 Lowell Thomas Travel Journalism Awards. His food and travel pieces have medaled in the North American Travel Journalists Association Awards and eight times in the Travelers'

Tales Solas Awards, and have appeared in the *San Francisco Chronicle, BBC Travel, Gastronomica, Roads & Kingdoms, Transitions Abroad*, and *Perceptive Travel*, among others. His work was recently anthologized in *Adventures of a Lifetime: Travel Tales from Around the World*, released in January, 2015 by World Traveler Press.

Ann Dufaux taught for many years at Centre de Linguistique Appliquée, Université de Franche Comté in Besançon, France, and previously wrote only academic publications. Today she writes fiction, travel stories, and poetry. Her work has been published in *Vignettes & Postcards From Paris* and long-listed for Ireland's Fish Publishing Prize. She once traveled professionally and now for pleasure, and enjoys meeting people and learning languages in places around the world such as Vietnam, Greece, Tunisia, Mexico and Nicaragua. Ann is the mother of four, and enjoys reading, singing and Tai Chi. She and her husband recently completed 2,000 km on the Compostela Trail.

Claire Fallou writes articles, creative nonfiction pieces and personal essays on travel, culture and the economy. Her work has appeared in the *Financial Times, La Tribune, Paris Revisited*, and *Grand Ecart*, a website dedicated to cinema for which she covered the Cannes Film Festival in spring 2015. Two of her short pieces can be found in *Vignettes & Postcards From Paris*, a collection of writings from Shakespeare and Company Bookstore, edited by Anna Pook and writer Erin Byrne, who is now Claire's mentor. In 2011, Claire won the *Financial Times/*

The Economist Nico Colchester Award for aspiring journalists. Claire lives in Paris.

Jeff Greenwald is the author of six books, including T*he Size of the World* (for which he created the first internet travel blog), *Scratching the Surface and Snake Lake*, a memoir set in Nepal during the 1990 democracy revolution. The 25th anniversary edition of his *Shopping for Buddhas* was released in 2014. Jeff also serves as Executive Director of EthicalTraveler.org, a global alliance of travelers dedicated to human rights and environmental protection.

Clara Hsu is a mother, musician, purveyor of Clarion Music Center (1982-2005), traveler, translator and poet. A nominee for the Pushcart Prize in poetry in 2001, Clara's first book of poems, *Mystique*, received Honorable Mention at the 2010 San Francisco Book Festival. Other works include a book of short stories, *Babouche Impromptu and Other Moroccan Sketches*; and *The First to Escape*, a second book of poems published in 2014 by Poetry Hotel Press. "Hsu's poems are both entrance and egress, a welcoming and a bon voyage. . . ."— Christopher Bernard (*Synchronized Chaos Magazine.*) Clara's poetic activities include her unusual performance combining Chinese poetry with Asian traditional instruments. Since 2010 she co-hosts with John Rhodes the San Francisco Open Mic Poetry Podcast TV Show, a monthly program featuring poets in the Bay Area and beyond. www.clarahsu.com.

Kimberley Lovato is a writer, traveler, and Champagne drinker whose articles and essays have appeared in magazines and websites such as *National Geographic Traveler, American Way, Celebrated Living, Delta Sky, Every Day With Rachel Ray, Virginia Living,* the *San Francisco Chronicle,* BBC. com, travelandleisure.com, and many more. Her book, *Walnut Wine & Truffle Groves,* about the people and food of the Dordogne region of France, was the Lowell Thomas Award-winning book of 2012, and her personal essays have appeared in volumes 8, 9 and 10 of *The Best Women's Travel Writing* and have also received recognition from Travelers' Tales Solas Awards. www.kimberleylovato.com.

Sandy McCutcheon is a prolific writer, spending his medina mornings writing novels and updating Morocco's premier news resource for travelers and expats, *The View from Fez.* He is also the author of over twenty-two plays and many best-selling novels. *In Wolf's Clothing* was the runner up in the HarperCollins National Fiction Prize. He has been an award-winning radio host for several programs including the popular radio show Australia Talks Back. McCutcheon is actively involved in The Sacred Music Festival in Fez. www.riadzany. blogspot.com.

Rolf Potts has reported from more than sixty countries for the likes of *National Geographic Traveler, The New Yorker,* Slate. com, *Outside,* the *New York Times Magazine,* and the Travel Channel. He is the author of two travel books, *Vagabonding: An Uncommon Guide to the Art of Long-Term World*

Travel (Random House, 2003), and *Marco Polo Didn't Go There: Stories and Revelations from One Decade as a Postmodern Travel Writer* (Travelers' Tales, 2008). His online home can be found at rolfpotts.com.

MJ Pramik Mary Jean (MJ) Pramik, a coalminer's daughter and a great granddaughter of the Mongolian plain, is an author, writer, and poet. She has published in medical and science journals and mainstream publications such as *Good Housekeeping* and the *National Enquirer*. Currently at work on her first novel, *G.E.M. of Egypt*, MJ Pramik has won several Solas travel writing awards and been nominated for a national Pushcart Prize in poetry. She blogs about caring for earth's survival and travel science, specifically how climate change will affect travel, at DearEarth.net and FieldNotes.tips, both accessible at www.mjpramik.com.

Candace Rose Rardon is a writer and artist whose stories and sketches have appeared on sites such as *BBC Travel*'s Words & Wanderlust column, *AOL Travel*, *World Hum*, *Gadling*, and National Geographic Traveler's *Intelligent Travel* blog. Her travel blog, *The Great Affair*, has been featured in *The New York Times*. Candace's story, "Beneath the Almond Tree," won the Grand Prize at the 2012 Book Passage Travel Writers and Photographers Conference. Sketches by Candace are included in the new edition of *Vignettes & Postcards From Paris*.

Marguerite Richards is a California-based writer and consultant. She travels to understand cultural differences and the nuances that separate and bring us together at the same time, with the resolve to render that palpable through her writing. Her work has appeared in *The San Francisco Chronicle*, *National Geographic's The Plate*, *Somm Journal*, *The Tasting Panel Magazine*, *Fathom*, *Rendez-vous en France Magazine*, *Passion Magazine*, and *Adventure Collection*.

Mike Richardson is proprietor of the acclaimed, cross-cultural Café Clock in Fez, and former maître d' of the prestigious Wolseley and the Ivy restaurants in London. His restaurant, Scorpion House, perched on a hill in the ancient town of Moulay Idriss, offers exotic ambiance and traditional Moroccan cuisine with a creative and modern twist. Mike recently opened a new Café Clock in the Kasbah of Marrakech. www.cafeclock.com.

Gloria Lodato Wilson lives in New York City and is a professor at Hofstra University, NY. Her academic writing includes numerous journal articles and book chapters addressing the learning needs of students with disabilities. She is the lead author of *Teaching in Tandem: Effective Co-Teaching in the Inclusive Classroom*. Gloria's non-academic writing focus is primarily first-person short works, and she is the author of *Confessions of a Praying Atheist*, a collection of vignettes which follow her path through love, grief and life. Gloria enjoys exploring New York City, traveling and hiking.

Permissions

Photography and Art Credits

Cover—Omar Chennafi

Back Cover—Christina Ammon

Map of Morocco, Sketches—Anna Elkins

Introduction—Christina Ammon

Arrival—Omar Chennafi

Vignettes—Siddharth Gupta

Memory—Kimberley Lovato

Change—Siddharth Gupta

Cuisine—Siddharth Gupta

Quest—Siddharth Gupta

Tradition—Siddharth Gupta

Postcards—Siddharth Gupta

Wisdom—Omar Chennafi

Mystery—Omar Chennafi

Timelessness—Siddharth Gupta

Afterword (Hajj)—Anna Elkins

Reputation Books

CPSIA information can be obtained
at www.ICGtesting.com
Printed in the USA
FSOW01n0415050217
30349FS